FAIR WINDS

Helen Carras

A KISMET™ Romance

METEOR PUBLISHING CORPORATION
Bensalem, Pennsylvania

KISMET™ is a trademark of Meteor Publishing Corporation

First Printing March 1992.

ISBN: 1-878702-84-X

Printed in the United States of America

For my husband, Chris

HELEN CARRAS

Helen Carras had a rich childhood in an ethnically diverse New York City neighborhood. After college and graduate school, she taught English and then became a high school guidance counselor. A move to California ten years ago was the signal for her to start writing full time. The result is sixteen published novels with, hopefully, many more to come. Helen and her husband presently live on an island off Florida's west coast.

ONE

"Nine hundred dollars a month! For an efficiency on Eleventh Street." Eve Marsdon couldn't believe it. "You must be kidding."

But the real estate agent wasn't even smiling. This realty office was very modern—all chrome and putty-colored metal—and the middle-aged Mr. Drew carried out the color scheme with his putty-colored summer suit and shiny gray hair. The atmosphere was cold; so was Mr. Drew.

"I had an apartment in that neighborhood once," Eve told him. "My roommate and I paid three hundred. And it had a separate bedroom."

"That must have been a thousand years ago."

Were all New Yorkers given to hyperbole, or only real estate agents? "Seven, to be exact," she corrected. Though it did seem a long time ago, that exciting semester at New York University when she and Greta had shared an apartment in Greenwich Village. The following year, after college, Greta had returned to New York, where she'd gotten married, been divorced, and eventually remarried. Eve, with fond memories of the fast-paced, vibrant city, had returned to the small town in Maryland where she'd grown up.

7

Mr. Drew shrugged. "Seven years ago was another era. There's no such thing as a three-hundred-dollar rental today, not for a furnished apartment—and certainly not in Manhattan. New York rents have just soared." He smiled smugly.

Sure, he could afford to smile, Eve thought resentfully. High prices meant extravagant commissions. He probably lived on Fifth Avenue.

"Soared is the right word," she said dryly. "Right into the stratosphere." Eve could afford the tuition for her sculpture class at the New School, but these astronomical rents would bankrupt her. Still, did she have a choice? She couldn't keep sleeping on that couch. The loft studio that Greta and George Avedon inhabited was one big open space; their bed was ten feet from the couch Eve had slept on. Eve and Greta had kept up their friendship during the six years since graduation from college, but friendship went just so far. A recently married couple needed privacy. And Eve needed a good night's sleep. George and Greta went in for molded plastic furniture and that couch, even padded with three inches of foam rubber, had been murder to sleep on. This was not the way she had expected to start her summer in New York.

"You ought to consider that six-month sublet," Mr. Drew said. "It's a steal at seven hundred."

"But I'm only here for the summer." Her art course was a six-week proposition, and she had planned to tack two weeks of pleasure on to either end. The pleasure part was eluding her. *This* end was not working out. "Isn't there anything else?" she asked, looking hopefully at the computer on his desk.

Mr. Drew clicked his nail against the almost-blank screen. "This is just a machine, not a magic box."

She looked crestfallen.

In a softened tone, he added, "Check with me in a few days. Something may come up." His voice said he doubted it. "When do you need it for?"

"Yesterday."

His impatience rose again. "Really! You should have started looking months ago. Why do out-of-towners feel they can get an apartment on an hour's notice?"

Eve bristled. "I'm not that naive. I *had* a sublet, but it fell through."

"Didn't you have a lease . . . a firm commitment?"

"This was a friend of a friend."

He sniffed. "One of those! Very unreliable."

So Eve had learned—the hard way. George Avedon's sister's brother-in-law had an efficiency in Gramercy Park which Eve was supposed to sublet. He was going to spend the summer in Cape Cod with his rich girlfriend. Then last week they'd had a fight and split up. His summer plans were canceled. Eve was determined not to cancel hers. Dammit, she'd been looking forward to this all year.

It wasn't that she didn't enjoy her work teaching and counseling students at Giles Junior College, but Leonardtown was a rural community and she had been promising herself this summer in the Big Apple for a long time.

She'd felt such a thrill driving into the city yesterday, so sure that she would find a place in a day or two. That was while her optimism was still intact. Manhattan had seemed as crowded and colorful and exhilarating as she remembered. Today, after six weary and futile hours of racing around following the leads in *The Times* real estate section, Eve also remembered that the city could be impersonal, hot, and exhausting. This was the third real estate office with the same discouraging, "We've-nothing-for-you" line. She had started this morning feeling as crisp and bright as her yellow linen dress—green eyes flashing, black hair a shiny aureole around her eager face, a spring in her long-legged stride. No longer. Her feet hurt, her shoulders drooped, and her dress was limp. Her spirits threatened to follow suit.

Mr. Drew's telephone rang. As he picked up the receiver, he smiled sarcastically and said, "Excuse me. This might be a new listing just perfect for you."

A cynical joke, but Eve listened anyway. If it was a listing, she would get first crack at it. Maybe her luck was changing.

"Oh, Professor Fraser," the agent said. "I've been expecting your call. I told the Gilligans they could move in any time after tomorrow, but I need the keys . . . Yes, I'll be around for at least another hour. Oh, yes, I did ask if they were interested in using your boat for a nominal fee, but they said no. Mrs. Gilligan said a rowboat taxed all her navigational skills. A cabin cruiser that sleeps four people is more than they care to tackle." He gave a little laugh.

"Nominal fee . . . sleeps four," Eve whispered, then suddenly cried out, "If it has a bed, I'll take it."

Mr. Drew was so startled he almost dropped the phone.

"It was the wildest kind of lucky break," Eve said excitedly. She was sitting with Greta and George around the small table in the kitchenette part of their studio.

George was listening with affable interest, but his wife wore her usual wary expression. The two were a contrast in looks and in temperament. George was large, blond, and easygoing. Greta was wiry, with a sharp face, frizzy hair, and a lot of nervous energy. She was also quick to form opinions and had no hesitancy in voicing them. Eve loved her friend, but didn't always appreciate the advice Greta so freely offered.

Eve described her adventures that morning, the futile running around and then overhearing the conversation between Mr. Drew and Professor Fraser. "That was the lucky part. Two hours later, I had a firm lease on the *Six Pack.*"

"On what?" George asked.

"The *Six Pack.* That's the name of the boat." Eve laughed as she recalled the scholarly-looking older man she had just met. "You'd think a classics professor would name his boat something like *Circe* or the *Naiad*. I think the name was on the boat when he got it."

"Just where's this thing parked?" Greta asked suspiciously.

"One does not say 'parked' about a boat," George told her.

"What does one say, smarty?"

George hesitated, so Eve answered. "Tied up—that's what one says. Dr. Fraser said the boat's tied up at a marina on the Hudson River. Four hundred for the whole summer for a Manhattan address. Can you believe it?"

"No," Greta said flatly.

At first, Professor Fraser hadn't taken Eve's offer seriously. She had talked to him briefly on the phone, but it was only after he'd come down to the real estate office that she had convinced him. Since he was spending the summer teaching at McGill University in Montreal, he wouldn't be using his boat. He'd offered it to the Gilligans, why not to her? Couldn't someone live on the *Six Pack*? Dr. Fraser did, he admitted, for weeks at a time. But only when he was cruising. "But there'll be less wear and tear this way," Eve had coaxed. "This'll be good for you, me, and the *Six Pack*." Dr. Fraser came around. Many people at the marina did live aboard their boats, and having someone on board would discourage theft and vandalism. They shook hands and the deal was made. Mr. Drew had looked on disbelievingly. Greta wore the same kind of look right now.

"Are you nuts?" she asked. "A boat is not an apartment."

"An apartment is not an apartment, either. The affordable vacant Manhattan apartment is as extinct as the dinosaur."

"Something will turn up. You can stay here until—"

"No way," Eve interrupted. "I love you both, but this place does not lend itself to communal living."

"You've got a point," George said.

Greta shot him a warning look. "But a boat! Eve, you don't know anything about boats."

"Hey, I've lived near water all my life."

"Near the water is not the same as *on* the water."

"I've been on the Chesapeake Bay. My father took me fishing lots of times."

Greta wasn't buying. "How many?"

"At least three." Eve didn't add that they'd fished from a fifteen-foot open boat with a small outboard, and that she'd been about twelve at the time. She was a good swimmer, loved the water, but just hadn't been around boats much. In this situation, it really shouldn't matter.

"That hardly makes you a boat expert," Greta said.

"Look, I'm just going to sleep on the boat, not take her on an ocean voyage."

"Suppose you get seasick."

"How can I?" Eve was prepared to counter every objection. "The boat's tied to a dock."

Greta tried a new approach. "Won't you be frightened? All alone?"

"I've lived alone for years." Three years, to be exact. Graham had died three years ago last month. They'd had less than two years together.

"That's different. In Leonardtown, you have neighbors."

"I'm not going to be the only one over there. Other people live on boats."

"That's in California."

Eve laughed. "Here, too. Right on Eighty-sixth Street. Now, stop fussing. I can take care of myself." Her firm tone must have been convincing because Greta backed off.

Eve appreciated her friend's concern, but she was an independent woman and made her own decisions. Her husband's death from leukemia had been shattering, even though expected. She and Graham had made the most of their short time together and Eve had never regretted her decision to marry him. How could one regret sharing love? Eve missed that sharing.

She had kept her promise to Graham that she would go on with her life. It hadn't been easy. His illness and care had so dominated her life; at first she'd felt numb and strangely adrift, acknowledging only her grief and loss. Gradually Eve's natural resiliency had taken over, leading her out of deep mourning. Her work with young people helped, plus her natural curiosity and artist's sensitivity to life and beauty.

There was, however, an area in her heart that had remained tightly closed. By choice, she'd avoided emotional and sexual intimacy. But recently she'd felt dissatisfied, vaguely acknowledging a void in her life. Eve had good memories of her marriage, but at twenty-seven, she was beginning to feel the need of something more substantial than memories. Perhaps even someone new in her life.

In the morning, when George went out to pick up some bagels, Eve tried to ease Greta's concern. "Stop worrying," she told her friend jokingly. "I'm really looking forward to this. I might even meet some handsome skipper at the marina."

"And you'd probably give him short shrift just as you have every man you've met lately," Greta said.

"Hey, there was no loss with any of them." Eve might be ready to love again, but the men she'd met had a different definition of love and sharing. They were more than willing to share a bed, but not themselves. And from what she had seen, there wasn't that much to share. Eve had never been tempted into a short-term affair.

"What was wrong with Randy Ames?" Greta had met Randy when she was in Leonardtown last Christmas. "I really thought he was your type."

"And what's that?" Eve herself didn't know.

"Oh, handsome and domineering. You certainly don't go for the wimp type."

"There must be some happy medium. Greta, you know what Randy had the nerve to tell me? That I appealed to him because I wasn't aggressive like some modern, so-called liberated females who try to dominate men."

"Is that why you dusted him off?"

"Darn right," Eve said briskly. "I certainly don't want a man who has to prove his masculinity by lording it over some female."

"Come on. He wasn't that bad. Y'know, you're never going to find the perfect man."

"I'm not looking for perfection."

"What then?"

Eve gave an exasperated laugh. "Nothing then. How did we get on this topic anyway? Look, this is just a summer vacation, not a romantic quest. Okay?"

Her friend shrugged. "If you say so."

Greta had planned a get-together with some other college friends, so it was after four when Eve finally got away. George carried her suitcase down. Eve made a point of traveling light: casual clothes in one twenty-four-inch suitcase, some books, and a carton containing her sculpting tools. Unfortunately, the stone she had bought for the sculpture class weighed thirty pounds. George grunted as he shifted it to make room for her suitcase in the trunk of her Volvo.

"I hope this is worth it," Greta said.

"It will be. I'm going to shape that piece of alabaster into something beautiful." Eve looked forward to long summer days on the boat when she could chip away on her stone. Classes were supposed to be three hours a week, but the class time was very flexible and she understood that many students worked on their own.

"I wasn't referring to your rock," Greta said.

"What then?"

"This whole escapade."

"Still think I'm nuts?"

"Yup. Unless luck's with you and you do get to meet some nautical Apollo to make it all worthwhile."

The first man Eve encountered at the marina was far from a nautical Apollo. Nautical, yes. The elderly proprietor who also took care of the marine supplies store wore a Greek fisherman's cap, a striped jersey, and navy bell bottom pants. He was easily two hundred forty pounds, much of it billowing about his middle. Apollo? No way. He looked as hot as Eve felt. It must be ninety degrees, she thought, and it wasn't even July yet. And where was the sea breeze? The magazine pictures of people on boats always showed them with their hair blowing in the breeze.

Eve introduced herself. "I'm Eve Marsdon. Dr. Fraser, Al Fraser, told me to ask for Mr. Slater."

"Reckon you've found him. You the lady's gonna take over the *Six Pack*?"

"That's me. Dr. Fraser said you'd give me the keys, Mr. Slater."

"Bo," he corrected. "Everyone around here calls me Bo." A smile creased his round cheeks. With a beard, he'd look like a nautical Santa. "Al called this morning. Said you'd be by, but I wasn't sure when. Lucky you got here now 'cause I was set to close for the day."

He did just that, following Eve out of the store and locking the door behind them. By the time Eve returned from her car with her suitcase, he had disappeared. Lucky, he'd said. Eve didn't feel very lucky. The heat was melting her enthusiasm. The paisley silk shirtwaist she had worn for Greta's party was now plastered to her lithe body. Why hadn't she taken the time to change? High-heeled patent-leather sandals were woefully unsuited to the gravelly parking area, and even less so to the wobbly wooden dock which led to where Bo Slater had said the *Six Pack* was berthed. The suitcase didn't help. It felt like it weighed a ton.

According to Bo, the *Six Pack* was in a slip down at

the far end. "I moved it this morning so you'd be where the regulars are," he'd explained.

Just my luck, she grumbled to herself. *The irregulars are probably closer*.

She stepped gingerly onto a floating dock and almost lost her balance. Suddenly Eve started to laugh. What an incongruous picture she presented in her silk dress and high heels. And carrying a Diane Von Furstenburg suitcase, no less. She should be in a T-shirt and jeans with a duffel bag slung over her shoulder. It *was* funny.

Then she saw him, the rugged-looking man standing on the deck of a large sailboat. She didn't blame him for looking at her curiously. She must be an odd sight dressed as she was and laughing to herself.

"I'm looking for the *Six Pack*," she called cheerily, her usual good humor reasserting itself.

He gestured to the boat on the other side of his. "Right here." That was it. No introduction or offer to help her with her bag. So much for dockside chivalry. Eve trudged by him.

There it was. No mistake. It read *Six Pack* right on the stern. Eve's optimism started to waver. It was pretty enough, a trim little cabin cruiser with a teak deck. But it seemed so *small*. The beamy sailboat next to it was almost twice as long. Eve had expected something more spacious. But of course, Al Fraser had talked about "roughing it".

Eve put down her suitcase and eyed the *Six Pack* warily. Its stern was swaying gently at least three feet from the dock. She looked at the stranger on the boat alongside.

"Isn't there a gangplank or something?" she asked.

A smile creased his tanned face. "Hardly. She's not the *Queen Mary*."

He didn't have to be sarcastic. "I can see that," she said crossly, "but how do I get onto the thing?"

His smile broadened, softening the hard contours of his face. "Pull the lines."

"The what? Lines?"

"The ropes. You'll pull her in closer."

Eve pulled and the *Six Pack* slid close, but when she stepped onto the stern, the boat was already drifting out again so she almost lost her balance.

"Better get out of those shoes," he called.

"Thanks, but I'm all right now."

"The deck won't be if you don't take off those spikes."

"Oh." Obviously, the deck was more important than she was. She kicked off her sandals. "I'm not used to boats, but I guess that's obvious."

"I gathered that when ,ou called the boat a 'thing.'"" He was giving her such an obvious once-over that Eve didn't bother to disguise her own scrutiny. This man wasn't handsome in the ordinary sense but had a compelling quality. He was about five ten, lean and muscular. The white T-shirt and faded jeans stretched tautly over a body which signaled balance and strength. There was strength, too, in the rather large features and prominent bone structure of his face. Dark unruly hair fell over his brow. Eve wished she could see the color of his eyes, but the afternoon sun was blurring her vision. Late thirties, she guessed, though that insolent smile had a rakish, youthful quality.

His scrutiny was long and thorough. He had stepped up on his side deck for a better view. Standing that way, one hand on the rigging and perfectly balanced, he looked as if he belonged there. But at sea—not on a boat tied to a dock. Eve raised both hands to shield her eyes, unaware that the gesture outlined the generous contours of her breasts.

"I'm Eve Marsdon," she said, and waited. She finally had to ask, "And you?"

"Vic Adesso."

"How do you do? I'm not trespassing, you know. I'm renting the *Six Pack* from Dr. Fraser."

"I know. He warned me you were coming."

"Warned?" Eve frowned at his choice of words. "I'm not a threat."

His eyes scanned her figure again. "I wonder."

That smile of his was maddening. Was he coming on to her? She usually discouraged instant flirtations. Too many men wanted to jump from introduction to invitation to consummation, a fast progression that she found distasteful. Was Vic Adesso going to be like the others? Somehow she didn't think so.

Briskly, she said, "It looks like we're going to be neighbors, at least until Dr. Fraser comes back. That *is* your boat, isn't it? I didn't notice the name. What do you call her?"

"Yes, she's mine—and I call her *Hippolyta*."

"Queen of the Amazons? That's a strange name for a boat."

"Why? Strong and tough . . . that's how I want my boat."

"Hippolyta was also a woman." Now why had she said that? His widening grin told her what was coming next.

"I like my women . . ."

Eve didn't let him finish. "I get the drift." She changed the subject. "Do you live aboard?"

"Yes, when I'm in town."

Would he be in town this summer? Did it matter? With a sudden awareness, she realized that it did. "I have to admit I'm a bit nervous about this," she said.

"Then why're you doing it?"

"It beats paying a fortune to rent a place in the city for the summer. Why are you doing it?"

"I like boats."

A sensible enough answer. Eve was beginning to feel foolish. "Well, I'd better take a look at the inside and get myself settled. See you later."

"Sure." He watched as she fumbled with the key and finally got the door to the cabin open. She had to duck under the entrance hatch to go down the two steps into the cabin.

She looked around with a sinking feeling. It wasn't the hot, stale smell that bothered her. She could air out the tiny room quickly enough. What she couldn't do was make it bigger. It had looked small from the outside, but the truth was it was downright Lilliputian. The ceiling hovered a few inches over her head. As she stood in the middle, her left hip touched the built-in dinette and her right thigh grazed against the cabinets on the other side.

On the counter was a two-burner stove. Eve opened a cabinet door and saw some basic cooking and eating utensils. Beyond the cabinets was a bench, too small to be called a couch, and under the forward part of the boat, V bunks. She opened a narrow door and found a toilet. Thank goodness! She could wash up at the small sink, but if there was no shower in the marina, she was in trouble. Well, what had she expected? As Vic had pointed out, this wasn't the *Queen Mary*. The sarcastic wretch! The *Hippolyta* was a much bigger boat. *He* probably had a full bathroom.

Eve searched for the refrigerator and finally opened the door to a small icebox. She would have to lug ice down from that machine on the dock. Eve groaned and then looked up to see Vic Adesso peering at her from the doorway.

"Is that why it's called the *Six Pack*?" she asked wryly. "Because that's all this icebox can hold?"

Vic handed her suitcase down to her. "It's fine for one person. One *man*, that is."

"Not for a woman?"

"We'll see," he said with a grin. "Good luck." Then he disappeared.

Infuriating! Eve squared her shoulders. Was he daring her? She'd show him she could manage just fine. She'd start by brewing herself a cup of tea. Eve found a tea bag and a kettle and stopped short. How did these so-called appliances work? She turned the spigot over the little sink but nothing happened. And the stove? Should she turn one of those dials? She'd probably blow up the place. Tomorrow she could ask Bo Slater for a crash course on how to operate everything. But what about right now?

In the country, neighbors helped one another. Eve marched up on deck and resolutely called, "Mr. Adesso. Mr. Adesso. Vic . . . ?" Had he left? She sighed with relief when he emerged.

"I'm sorry to bother you, but could you spare a few minutes to show me how things work here. I'd rather not resort to trial and error with someone else's property."

Vic nodded approvingly, stepped onto the dock, and deftly leaped aboard the *Six Pack*. She envied the sure grace of his movements. Eve wobbled with every shifting motion of the deck under her. "That's very sensible," Vic said when he joined her. At least he didn't sound surprised that she showed some sense. "I should have thought of it," he added. "Sorry."

"Why should you have thought of it. I'm not your responsibility. But I would appreciate your help."

He followed her into the cabin. "I'll show you how the head works first," he said. When he maneuvered to get by, their bodies touched.

"Makes for real togetherness, doesn't it?" she quipped, and was instantly sorry. The cramped space had them so close she felt his breath on her face and could count the quickening pulse beats in his throat. She looked up; his eyes were gray, shining with a peculiar intensity. Eve knew her closeness affected him. For a second, he held his breath, then his nostrils flared as he drew in air. What was she doing? She had just met this man. The last thing she wanted was to have him think she was coming on to him. She managed an awkward laugh and said, "You're right about this being suitable for one person only. Now, show me how my head works—whatever that is."

He laughed, a nice sound. "*Your* head's still a mystery to me—but I can explain about the *Six Pack's*."

The head, she discovered, was the toilet, and Vic showed her how it worked and how to pump the water in. Then he demonstrated the gas stove, and plugged the *Six Pack* into the dockside electricity. He removed the support column from under the dinette table and lowered it to seat level where it rested on cleats. With foam cushions, he turned it into a bed.

Eve was delighted. "That's great. I'd have nightmares if I had to sleep in those V bunks."

"You *are* nervous, aren't you?"

"That was a joke," she said defensively. "Don't worry. You won't hear me screaming for you in the middle of the night."

"Oh? Too bad." He looked down at her for a long moment.

Eve noticed that his head just cleared the low ceiling of the cabin. "You're going to have a flat top," she said.

"What?"

"Your hair . . . You're so tall, the ceiling's flattening your hair."

"Is it?" He smiled. "That's a non sequitur."

"So?"

"So nothing."

It was the confined space that imparted this air of intimacy, Eve thought. Anything a man said sounded suggestive if it was uttered inches away from you. Of course, Vic *was* a very attractive man. This close his masculinity was extra potent. Eve had been alone for a long time—perhaps too long.

Suddenly Vic backed away onto the steps leading to the deck. Cheerfully, and impersonally, he said, "You should be all right. For tonight anyway."

"Oh, sure. And thank you."

"Don't mention it." He gave a slight wave and disappeared.

TWO

Eve was annoyed. What had Vic meant by "for tonight anyway"? Did he think she wasn't going to stick it out? Well, Mr. Victor Adesso could just think again. Eve opened her suitcase and started to cram her things into the few storage spaces. Not everything fit. She could leave some things in the suitcase. She'd manage.

She looked around the cabin. What was the big deal? So it wasn't a luxurious stateroom. Sure, it was small, but then she hated doing housework anyway. In minutes she had talked herself into an optimistic mood. She changed into comfortable, worn jeans, a plaid cotton blouse, and sneakers. She would go find that grocery store she had passed on West End Avenue and pick up some basic provisions. Al Fraser had warned her that the larder was pretty bare.

When Eve returned almost an hour later, she found a chunk of ice in the icebox. It must have been Vic. But she had locked up; that meant he had a key. Maybe he took care of Al Fraser's boat in the older man's absence. Where she lived, neighbors looked out for each other's houses. It was the same thing, wasn't it?

She could ask him for the key, but that would be awkward. His getting the ice for her had been a neighborly gesture. Besides, intuition told her that Vic would never use that key to intrude on her. Her earlier annoyance was gone. Eve realized that she had really been angry with herself, confused by her sudden attraction to this man, and had displaced her annoyance on to him.

Whoa, she cautioned. Meeting a good-looking guy didn't constitute a romance, especially when he seemed to look on her as a nuisance and a klutz.

Eve made herself a sandwich and took it on deck along with a cup of coffee. She was disappointed at the lack of activity next door. Had Vic gone out? She couldn't help wondering about him. Did he work? He must have money to afford that big boat. Did he have a house someplace? A wife maybe? *I hope not*, she thought, then cautioned herself that it shouldn't matter. Still . . .

She knew nothing about Vic Adesso—but wanted to. There was something challenging about him, provoking her interest and curiosity. Eve had met attractive men before, but this heightened physical awareness was something she hadn't experienced in a long time. It confused her.

Finally, she went below and fixed up her bed. She felt restless lying there until she looked out and saw a light go on in the cabin across the way. As the gentle rocking of the boat lulled her to sleep, Eve dismissed her misgivings. Living aboard the *Six Pack* might be roughing it, but she had a feeling that it would be worth it.

Vic Adesso was also restless that night. He usually read for an hour or two before trying to sleep, but tonight he couldn't concentrate on his book. Thomas Hardy's sultry heroine, Eustacia Vye, was less intriguing than the young woman on the *Six Pack*. Quite a change from Al. He smiled. Certainly a helluva lot prettier. But she could be a problem . . . make demands on him. Eve Marsdon obviously knew nothing about boats.

Vic was serious about sailing. He never let it interfere with his work, but it was more than a hobby. Boats were his passion. Maria had once told him that he had two obsessions, his business and sailing. But it was a good-humored observation, without rancor. And Maria Spezia had her own obsession, but she was fortunate enough to be able to combine work and play. A tennis pro could do that. Maybe that was why they'd never married; each had other consuming interests. Their long affair had settled into an affectionate camaraderie that suited them both. Maria didn't sail with him often. Unless they were racing, she became bored. But she was a trained athlete and knew how to crew. Not like most women. He remembered that redhead last year who'd pretended she loved to sail. He'd let her come along on a race out of City Island and she had ended up in the water and he had ended up coming in last.

This Eve Marsdon could be another such helpless female. Helpless? Vic recalled her show of spirit, the flash of fire in her green eyes, the springiness of the black curly hair, the texture of which tempted an exploration by his fingertips. The word "helpless" didn't suit her. There was an eagerness about her, a sense of life springing from an inner core that gave her an appealing vitality. Very different from Maria's forceful drive. And very attractive. He remembered how being close to her had aroused him.

Dangerous, he warned himself. Al Fraser had told him Eve Marsdon was a pretty schoolteacher from a little town in Maryland. "A nice young woman," he had said. In other words, not the kind one fools around with.

So why was he so tempted?

Eve was surprised that she had slept so soundly. The night breeze had cooled the cabin and her bed was surprisingly comfortable. Even the sounds of the lines straining with the movement of the boat and the lapping of water against the hull had been soothing.

Maybe I'm not such a landlubber after all, she thought as she washed. The tiny mirror above the sink didn't encourage elaborate makeup rituals, which suited Eve just fine. She brushed her short curls into a haphazard but attractive halo, put on the jeans and cotton shirt she had worn the night before, and made herself breakfast. Juice, a bowl of cereal, a cup of coffee. That would do fine. A little leery of starting the gas stove, she wasted three matches before getting it going, but soon had the kettle boiling. Eve tried not to think about the modern electric efficiency of her kitchen back home.

Carrying her breakfast outside on deck, Eve made a mental note to buy a couple of tray tables. For the time being, she improvised, using an upside-down bucket as a makeshift table. She'd also need a coffeepot. This morning she had to settle for instant coffee.

Actually, it tasted pretty good. Perhaps because of the fresh morning air. It was hard to believe that she was actually in New York City. She was glad her course didn't start for almost two weeks. This was too nice to leave. If only all mornings were like this. But what would she do if it rained? She had her books and the cassette player in the car, but being confined to the cabin wouldn't be much fun. Of course, there was always the city and its countless attractions. Eve's eyes strayed to the boat across from her and knew that her interests were focused more on the immediate environment.

She remembered the excitement Vic had engendered in her. Would it be the same today? She became impatient to find out. Wasn't he ever getting up? How long could she sit here nursing her cup of coffee? She saw his cabin door swing open. Good. Her mental telepathy was working.

The smell of freshly brewed coffee preceded him. "Good morning," she called when he came on deck. "Mmm . . . your coffee smells heavenly." Not exactly a subtle hint.

He looked at the cup in her hand. "Better than yours?"

She nodded. "I don't have a coffeepot, and instant's just not the same."

He disappeared and came back with an old-fashioned metal percolator. Lightly, he stepped onto the finger slip separating the two boats and reached over to hand her the coffeepot. "Help yourself," he offered. "You can keep the pot if you like."

That wasn't what Eve had in mind. She made no move to take it. "Come on board. We can both have a second cup."

He hesitated, but the alternative would be to set the pot unceremoniously down on the deck. He didn't have to pull the boat closer as he spanned the space from the dock with an easy leap of his long legs. She could see the play of muscles under the tan poplin pants. Beneath the surface of nonchalance, Eve sensed a restrained power. So different from Graham's gentle power. Is that what attracted her? She noticed Vic was more formally dressed today, with a short-sleeved yellow shirt open at the neck. Incongruously, however, he was barefoot.

He saw her looking at his feet. "I didn't expect to come calling," he said with a grin. "I haven't finished dressing yet."

"I guess you don't need shoes around here."

"But you do in town, and I have business in the city this morning."

Eve was disappointed. "What kind of business?" Now what on earth made her ask as if she had a right to know? "Excuse me," she blurted with embarrassment. "None of my business, of course. I've got this awful curiosity." Suddenly she noticed that he was still holding the coffeepot. "Here, let me take that." She almost grabbed it out of his hands. What had gotten into her? Why was this man able to fluster her so? "Can I get you some breakfast? Some cereal, maybe? That's about all I was willing to chance this morning. I'll have to get more experience with the galley before I'm ready to whip up any gourmet delights."

"No, thanks. Coffee's all I take in the morning."

She hoped she could pour them each a cup without spilling any. She did. "At least sit down," she invited.

"For a minute." Vic looked at his watch. "I've got to be at the Equitable Building by nine."

"Too bad you have to leave this nice breeze. I hope the city won't be too hot today."

He smiled. "I'll probably be back before it heats up."

Thinking, but not saying, *That's good*, Eve sipped her coffee. "Yesterday was a scorcher."

He nodded.

She took another sip. "Good coffee."

"Thank you."

Well, she had exhausted the weather and the coffee as topics of conversation. Eve hadn't felt this awkward with a man for a long time, not since she'd met and fallen in love with Graham so many years ago. Suddenly she smiled broadly.

"Something funny?" Vic asked with a quizzical look.

"Me. Because I'm trying to make conversation to keep you here."

The unexpected confession surprised him. "Well I'm flattered—I think." The gray eyes took on a glint like shining pewter. "But I do have to go. My appointment . . ."

"Of course."

When he stood, Eve tried to hand him the coffeepot.

"No, you finish it up."

"Thanks. Next time I'll try to make my conversation more scintillating," Eve said, smiling up at him.

"No need."

With that he stepped off the *Six Pack*, across the dock, and onto his own boat, where he disappeared into the cabin.

Eve sat for a moment, puzzling over the "No need".

Did that mean she was scintillating enough, or did it mean not to bother? *Come on now, lady*, she scolded herself. *Stop trying to analyze every word and look from this Vic Adesso. Whatever is, is; and what will be, will be. How's that for a comforting platitude?*

But Eve did not really believe that fatalistic saying. In fact, she usually argued against such a philosophy with the students she counseled. "You have to decide what you want, plan how to get it, and execute your plan," was what she urged. Young people were often so afraid of failing that they abdicated control and left their future to chance. If things went wrong, they could blame fate instead of themselves.

That had never been Eve's style. However, it had been a long time since she had wanted anything really important—or *anyone*.

In less than five minutes, Vic reappeared. A brown lightweight sports jacket made his shoulders looked even broader. The dark hair was combed back, but Eve guessed it wouldn't stay in place very long. Stepping onto the dock, Vic pointed to his brown loafers.

"Shoes . . . I'm dressed for civilization now."

"Too bad. You looked more comfortable before." She smiled, adding, "I liked you better the other way."

"I don't think my bankers would agree. See you."

Eve watched him make his way down the dock to the parking area. He stopped for a moment to talk to Bo Slater, and both men looked her way. Then Vic got into a silver-gray Jaguar and drove off.

His bankers, he had said. Bankers in the plural. And that Jaguar. Obviously Vic Adesso was not a penniless boat bum. But just what was he? Again an endless stream of questions came to Eve's mind. She sat for a long time until she suddenly realized that her coffee was cold, and a bee was exploring the drying flakes left in her cereal bowl. It would be embarrassing if she forgot all about time and Vic was to return and find her sitting exactly where he'd left her. *Get with it*, she told herself.

In less than an hour, Eve had cleaned and had the cabin organized. At least she'd never get tired from wasted steps and housework, she thought as she stood in the middle of the cabin. She could almost touch every corner without moving. The windows looked a bit grimy and the counter surfaces and walls would benefit from a polishing cleaner, but those chores could wait. If Vic returned soon, she didn't want to look like an obsessive housewife.

What did she want to look like?

A free spirit, she decided. A woman who belonged on a boat, not one who had to be told to remove her spiked heels.

She had promised to call Greta this morning and knew she'd better do it before her friend started worrying. The last thing Eve wanted was for Greta to come charging down to the marina to rescue her. There were public phones right outside the store.

"You mean you actually slept on that thing?" Greta asked after Eve had given her a brief rundown.

"Of course. And don't call it a 'thing,' " Eve said, and repeated Vic's comment. "A boat is not a thing."

"Well, get you. Twenty-four hours adrift and suddenly you're an oceangoing old salt."

Eve had to laugh. "The *Six Pack*'s tied to a dock, not adrift, and the Hudson's a river, not an ocean."

"Whatever," said Greta crossly. "Sure you don't want to be rescued yet?"

"Quite sure. And I don't like that word 'yet.' I am not going to need rescuing. Believe me, everything's fine. In fact, better than I thought. This is turning out to be very interesting."

Greta was suspicious. "Interesting—that's the adjective for when you can't think of something good to say. Sure you're not trying to put a bright side to a bad deal?"

"Quite sure," Eve said without hesitation. "I needed a change, something different in my life." For some reason, she chose not to mention Vic Adesso. She promised to stop by soon for a visit and said good-bye.

Bo Slater was standing in the doorway of the store. "Mornin', ma'am. Everything all right?" he asked.

"Just fine, Bo."

"Vic said for me to make sure you don't need nuthin'."

Why didn't Vic make sure himself? So that was why the two men were looking over at her earlier. At least he cared.

"I'm fine for now, thank you," she said.

"Some of the people here, they call for groceries down to Caruso's on Eighty-eighth. He delivers."

"That's good to know."

"Yeah. He brings everything over to the store here with everybody's order labeled, and then I toot my whistle three times and those who have orders can pick them up."

"Very convenient."

"Yeah, it works pretty good. Vic says you've got plenty of ice for now. When you're low, the machine's right over here. But don't you try to carry down no block of ice. When you need some, me or Vic'll do it."

"I wouldn't want to impose on either of you." Eve was determined to fend for herself, but liked the idea of Vic's being concerned.

"No sweat. I tease Vic how he makes a quarter on every block of ice we sell so he oughta do most of the hefting."

"How come he makes a quarter?"

"Well, he owns this place, don't he?"

"He does? I didn't know that."

"Yeah. He bought it from the previous owners, some corporation, when they were going to cancel all the leases to do a lot of renovation. Vic took it over and did the renovations without making anyone leave. He said it was easier than having to move out. Ain't he something?"

"He sure is." She would have liked to hear more about her intriguing neighbor, but Bo was called into the store to tend to some customers.

Eve wandered about to check out the marina's facilities. Everything was sparkling. The laundry room had new washers and dryers and even a folding table and rack to hang things. The ladies' washroom was well lighted and clean and she was pleased to see a shower stall in a room to the side. At least she wouldn't have to drive to the Avedons' apartment to take a shower.

She walked down onto the floating docks to investigate the different boats in the marina's slips. There were all kinds, most of them locked up on this weekday morning. There were sailboats and powerboats of all sizes. Eve paused before a particularly impressive yacht in the section where the largest boats were berthed. Sixty feet, at least. The deck was furnished as lavishly as a mansion's poolside patio.

"*My Weakness,*" she read aloud from the name emblazoned in gold script on the stern.

"Not my only one, unfortunately," someone said.

Eve was startled. She hadn't heard the man come up behind her.

"Sorry. Didn't mean to frighten you," he said.

He was a thin man of medium height with pleasant blue eyes, sandy hair, and sharp features. His green sport shirt was trimmed around the collar and pocket in the same electric blue as his pants. Even his boat shoes matched the outfit. Very dapper. He reminded her of Fred Astaire in costume, ready to break into a dance routine.

"I didn't hear you come up," she said. "I was just admiring this boat. Is she yours?"

His smile revealed small, even teeth. "Yep. That yacht's my weakness."

She caught the change of nouns. "When does a boat get to be a yacht?"

"When it's big enough."

Eve laughed. "Then I guess the *Six Pack*'s going to stay a boat. It shows no signs of growing."

"The *Six Pack*? That's Fraser's boat, isn't it? Did you just buy it?"

"Oh, no. I'm just using it for a few weeks." Eve explained her situation.

"Then you'll be around for a while. Wonderful," he said with enthusiasm and extended his hand. "I'm Glen Rader."

"Eve Marsdon." Why did people with such limp grips always want to shake hands, she wondered.

Glen held on a little too long and asked, "Single, married, divorced, or widowed?"

Eve resented the question, as she did the slightly caressing motion of his thumb. "The latter," she said abruptly, and pulled her hand free.

He was sensitive enough to catch her resentment. "Sorry. That may have sounded a bit crass."

"It did."

He cocked his head and gave her an appraising look. "You're direct. I like that. I am, too, which is why I asked about your marital status."

"Mr. Rader, we just met."

"It doesn't take me long to make up my mind about someone. I intend for us to get to know each other. And you can't persist with that Mr. Rader formality when I'm going to call you Eve. And I hope I'll be calling you quite often."

Well, this one was certainly no enigma. He made his interest quite evident. Glen Rader had a debonair kind of charm, and Eve couldn't help feeling flattered. "You certainly can't be pining for female companionship with an attraction like *My Weakness*. Not that you need any special attraction," she hastened to add.

He wasn't a bit offended. "I admit it helps. Better than etchings, don't you think?"

She wasn't going to answer that. "Do you live here?" she asked.

"Off and on when the weather's nice. Now that you're here, I may increase my 'on' periods."

"You don't waste any time, do you?"

His glance scanned her approvingly, lingering on her full breasts which thrust against the thin plaid shirt. "I try not to. Would you like to come aboard and explore *My Weakness*?"

Eve was more amused than annoyed. "Thank you, no. Another time, maybe. I have something I must do." Like go back and wait for Victor Adesso to return.

"Before you go . . . I'm throwing a party here Thursday night, kind of launching the summer season, don't you know. Can you make it? Just fifty or so intimate friends and all the marina regulars. Inevitably we spill out all over the dock, so it's best to invite everybody. You'll come?"

"Why not?" Since *everybody* would be there.

"Great." Glen looked genuinely pleased. "But look, you don't have to wait until Thursday. I'm here all day today. If you start to get claustrophobic on that cramped little boat, come over for a visit."

"She's not that little or cramped," Eve said defensively, and then wondered at this sense of loyalty to the *Six Pack*. "And I don't feel at all claustrophobic." Walking away, she sensed Glen Rader's eyes on her, probably on her derriere. Eve suppressed the desire to affect an exaggerated wiggle as a joke, but Glen might misinterpret the gesture.

At the store, Bo introduced Eve to Fran and Lou Rosario who lived on a small houseboat. "Welcome to the neighborhood," Fran said with a warm smile. They were in their twenties, both in graduate school, and loved living on their houseboat. Fran was a fragile-looking blonde, and her tall, swarthy husband towered over her. "Have you met everyone yet? The regulars, I mean?" Fran asked.

"Just Vic Adesso and Glen Rader."

"Ah, our two eligible bachelors," Fran said with a giggle.

So Vic wasn't married!

"Semi-eligible, in Vic's case," Lou added.

Now what did he mean by that?

Fran spread her hands helplessly. "And they say women gossip. Come on, Lou. We've got a nine-thirty class."

Stay . . . gossip . . . tell me what's going on, Eve wanted to protest. But of course she didn't.

Back on the *Six Pack*, Eve made herself a sandwich. She almost stabbed herself trying to chip off a piece of ice for her iced tea. Her morning cheerfulness was gone. Music, that's what she needed. Music with her meal. Eve went to her car to get her cassette player. She looked around the lot. No silver Jaguar.

Eve stretched lunch to more than an hour while she listened to her Fats Waller cassette. Then she went back to the car to unload her sculpture material. She couldn't do much work without more space and a table on which to set her stone, but she could study the piece of alabaster. So far, she hadn't been able to decide what to make of it. A peculiar shape, it didn't suggest any particular form. Eve had chosen it for the rich grains of pink and gold and mauve buried in its depths. She should have some form in mind before she went to her first class.

Bo was busy in the store so Eve took one of the red wagons kept on the dock and managed to lift the heavy box out of her car trunk and into the wagon. "First I almost stab myself and now I'm going to give myself a hernia," she muttered. "This is not my day." The wagon was designed as a child's toy and she felt a little silly pulling it down the dock.

The wagon almost got away from her when she hauled it over the bump at the head of her slip. Wasn't there a brake on the thing? She pulled it as close as she could and looked at the *Six Pack* bobbing comfortably three feet away. This was going to be tricky. She had to lift the heavy carton, pull the boat close, and get herself on board without falling in the drink. But how?

Twice she pulled the lines, but by the time she'd lifted the carton, the *Six Pack* had drifted away again. Disgusted, Eve wondered if her art was worth getting a hernia over. One more try. This time she lifted the heavy box first and then used her foot to pull on the line holding the boat. She prayed she wouldn't get her foot caught and lose her balance. When the boat edged close enough, Eve managed to step onto the stern. It was an awkward maneuver and she landed heavily, the sudden weight causing the boat to bounce. Eve teetered. Instinct prompted her to kneel and put the box down to avert tragedy. To her relief, it worked.

"Well done!"

The voice startled her. Eve turned. Vic was standing there, his feet apart for balance because Eve's movements had made the dock shake. He'd taken off the brown jacket which was slung over one shoulder and his shirt was plastered to his chest. Even in her confusion, Eve couldn't help admiring his arresting masculinity. But how long had he been standing there?

"Thanks for the after-the-fact compliment. A before-the-fact assist would have been more appreciated," Eve said crossly, trying to ignore the appeal of his lopsided smile.

He shrugged. "I wanted to see how you'd manage."

"Really?" Now she was annoyed. "Some kind of test? Did I pass?"

His grin broadened. "You did okay. What've you got in that box, anyway?"

"A rock," she snapped.

"Come again."

"A rock," Eve repeated loudly.

"That's what I thought you said." Vic's expression was quizzical. "Planning to sink a dead body?"

"Not a bad idea," Eve answered, giving him a venomous look.

Vic got the message. It made him laugh. The hearty sound disarmed her.

Eve dug into her jeans pocket, found the key, and opened the door to the cabin. Her awareness of Vic's continued perusal made her movements awkwardly self-conscious. She had the key ring looped over one finger and when she spun around to get her carton, it somehow swung off, flying through the air. It landed with an ominous splash.

"Oh, no!" she yelled and ran to look over the side. "Damn."

There it was in the water, held up by its flotation device, drifting toward the bow.

Vic had come up beside her. "Get the boat hook," he ordered.

"What?"

"Get the boat hook." When she didn't respond immediately, he added, "Unless you'd prefer to dive in after the key."

Eve didn't appreciate his sarcasm, but she needed his help. "What's a boat hook?"

"Over there under the seats . . . that pole with a hook on the end."

Eve rushed to get it and thrust the hook end at him.

"Easy," he cried. "You're trying to hook the key ring, not me."

This was not the time to debate that, Eve told herself as he shoved the pole into her hand. Apparently he expected her to use it. She tried. It was awkward, handling the long pole and guiding the hooked end through the water.

"Don't splash around," Vic warned. "You'll make waves and drive the thing away. Just ease the hook under the ring and lift."

Easier said than done. Each time she thought she had

it, the ring slipped off. Eve was afraid it would float out of reach. She leaned so far over the side that her feet lifted off the deck. Suddenly she felt Vic's hands holding her waist, pulling her back.

"Careful you don't go overboard with the keys," he cautioned. "You're not wearing a flotation device."

Eve tried to ignore the pressure of his hands but felt their warmth through her thin shirt. She stabbed again with the boat hook, succeeding only in pushing the bobbing key ring inches away.

"It's getting away from me. Hold on to me, Vic," she cried as she boosted herself farther out. With another pass and some laborious grunts, Eve finally hooked on to the metal ring.

"Hold it steady, Eve."

Vic was pulling her back. Her shirt had been dragged out of her jeans so his hands now circled her bare waist. In a few seconds, he had her standing upright, but her skin carried the imprint and warmth of his fingers. He stood behind her, lightly touching her shoulders, his voice directing her.

"Don't try to jerk it in, Eve. Just walk backward holding the pole steady until you can drop the key ring on the deck."

He walked backward, pulling her along. She couldn't help pressing against him as they moved. She felt the shape of his belt buckle, even the buttons on his shirt. The heat from his body entered hers, igniting deep inside her a glow which spread throughout her body. Eve's hands were quivering when she finally set down the pole with the key ring safely attached. Turning to face him, she stood so close that her breasts brushed against him. She heard his sharp intake of breath. Vic's hands, now clutching her arms, tightened their grip.

His face was so close. She read tension in his narrowed eyes and the strained lines of his mouth. Her palms against his chest picked up the pulsating rhythm of his heartbeat,

Eve's mouth was dry; she wet her lips with the tip of her tongue. If she lifted her face a few inches, her mouth would meet his. Vic's quick, shallow breath fanned her face. Her lips parted as he lowered his head. His fingers suddenly tightened—but to push her away, not draw her close. He stepped back, leaving her confused and strangely bereft.

Why had he pulled back? "I'm sorry to be such a bother," she said, hoping he would deny it. "If you hadn't come along, I'd never have gotten that key. Thanks." Her voice sounded shaky.

Vic had composed himself. "No thanks necessary," he said, picking up his jacket from where he'd tossed it.

"I don't know how it happened. The key ring just flew out of my hand. I seem to get clumsy when I'm not on solid ground."

"Hey, no sweat. Some people just aren't meant for boats."

Eve stiffened angrily. Was he putting her in that category? "Well, I don't think I'm one of them. I may be a novice now, but I'll learn."

"Whoa." Her vehemence surprised him. "Simmer down. You're the one said you were clumsy on boats."

"You didn't have to agree so readily. You don't know me yet, Mr. Adesso. Not by a long shot."

"So it seems," he said with a slightly mocking smile. "I hope I have something to look forward to. Excuse me. I think that's my phone ringing."

Before she could think of an appropriately clever reply, he disappeared into his cabin. After a while, she heard what sounded like the clicking of a typewriter or a computer coming from the *Hippolyta*. She didn't see Vic for the rest of the afternoon.

_____ THREE _____

Eve was restless after Vic had gone. She took back the wagon, got a Coke from the machine outside the store, and returned to the *Six Pack*. Vic was still inside. She took out her piece of alabaster and examined it. Moving it around on the sand-filled denim sack she used as a cushion, Eve looked for the angle that would suggest some format, some shape. But another shape kept insinuating itself into her consciousness, the strong, hard profile of Vic Adesso. Finally, sighing with frustration, she gave up. She was getting nowhere. She'd take another look tomorrow.

At dinnertime, Eve's hunger pangs indicated that she'd not be satisfied with a sandwich again. Pasta—that was it. She'd cook up some spaghetti for herself. The little stove could handle a pot of spaghetti and some meat sauce. An accomplished cook, Eve was well aware that the spaghetti she threw into the boiling water was too much for one person.

So I'll have leftovers, she told herself, choosing to forget that she hated leftover pasta. She had cut up an onion, browned it with chopped meat, and added a jar of Italian sauce. The pervasive spicy aroma, she was sure, had to be wafting across to her neighbor's cabin.

But Vic gave no sign of being tempted. Apparently he was working; there was still faint sounds from a computer or typewriter. So much for the old proverb about the way to a man's heart, Eve thought as she filled her plate. Maybe he didn't even like spaghetti. But with a name like Adesso, how could he not?

Well, she liked it and meant to enjoy her dinner. Eve poured a glass of red wine and settled herself at the dinette table. Halfway through her meal, she couldn't eat any more. What had happened to her usual hearty appetite?

She should be used to eating alone, but tonight was different. She felt lonely and resentful, and she knew why. It was because of that man over there, not twenty feet away, but it might as well have been twenty miles. Distance wasn't just a numerical measure, and Vic controlled the gap between them. Was he avoiding her? Did it have something to do with Lou Rosario's reference to Vic's being "semi-eligible"?

Giving up on eating, Eve cleared away her dish and made herself some fresh coffee. She took her cup on deck. The sun was setting behind the jagged skyline. There was a haze in the air and clusters of clouds were tinted pink and orange by the sun. Eve had always been excited by sunrises and sunsets, marveling as the day crossed from one dimension to its opposite. They symbolized change and renewal, the underlying continuity of life.

She heard Vic coming onto his deck. Without turning, she said, "Beautiful, isn't it?"

"Lots of clouds."

"Beautiful clouds."

"It'll be raining by morning."

She turned to look at him. "What a pessimist you are."

"I'm a realist. Those are rain clouds."

"Well, it's not raining yet so we can enjoy the evening. Come have some coffee. It's your pot."

"You're over your mad?"

She laughed. "Yes. It wasn't a real mad. I was annoyed at myself for presenting such a clumsy picture, and annoyed at you for believing it."

He cocked his head and seemed to study her, his gaze curiously intent. "What do you want me to believe?"

"That's a trick question. I'm not going to answer it." Partially because Eve wasn't sure of the answer. "How about that coffee?"

He hesitated, then said, "I really can't. I'm waiting for some reports to come in over the modem."

"I thought I heard a computer going."

"I have a love-hate relationship with that damn machine," Vic said ruefully, "but it does enable me to keep in touch with things."

"What kinds of things?" Her question was prompted by more than idle curiosity. There was much she wanted to know about Vic Adesso, and there was nothing *idle* about her interest in him.

"Warehouses . . . mini-storage setups. That's my business."

"I thought boats were your business."

He shook his head. "My pastime and my passion, but warehousing pays the bills. I have to go. See you."

Eve masked her disappointment. "Good night then. I'll return your coffeepot after I wash it."

"Keep it. I've another one."

"No. I don't like to borrow things." She was beginning to suspect that what she wanted from Vic Adesso couldn't be borrowed.

After Vic went below, Eve sat there until the sun disappeared. Could a person fall in love in twenty-four hours? Ridiculous! Why was she even thinking this way? She didn't believe in love at first sight, or second, or third. Not for a mature, lasting relationship.

But how about an immature, short-term romance? Eve gave a soft, breathless laugh. She had promised herself an exciting summer in New York, and if an exciting man could be part of that scenario, why not go for it? Just as long as she kept her wits about her and didn't let herself get hurt.

This kind of thinking was not like her—at least not like the person she'd been these last few years. But then, hadn't she decided it was time to change? Wasn't that behind her decision to come to New York? Perhaps this summer's experience would be the catalyst for a new phase in her life. She was going to be here for ten weeks, in close proximity to the only man who'd attracted her in years. *Stop analyzing and just enjoy*, she told herself.

Suddenly she felt good. She would take a hot shower and then settle down in her bunk with one of the romance novels she'd brought. Eve went below, took off her sneakers and shirt and jeans, and put on a wraparound white terry robe. She grabbed a towel and wash kit and headed for the shower room. It was now dark, but the dock was lighted. Eve was reminded of her sophomore year when she'd lived in one of the old dorms with the lavatories down the hall. But at college, she didn't have to go outside. What does one do in winter? she wondered. "One doesn't live on a boat in winter, dummy," she answered herself. Not a boat like the *Six Pack*. The *Hippolyta*? That might be different. She'd have to ask Vic about that.

The shower was just what she needed. After rinsing away her herbal-scented shampoo, Eve lingered, adjusting the shower head so the spray pelted her in an invigorating water massage. She loved the tingling bite of arrows of water striking her skin and the vigorous toweling she gave herself afterward. A sensuous person, Eve was acutely responsive to all kinds of sensations. She was sensitive to touch and textures, tuned in to her body's reactions.

Having neglected to bring fresh underwear, Eve tied her robe securely around her and headed back to the *Six Pack*. And why hadn't she remembered to wear her flip-flops? Now her feet would get dirty. Well, it couldn't be helped.

"Ouch!" The shoes would also have saved her from the splinter which caused her to yelp in pain as she neared the end of her dock. Eve dropped her towel and toiletry kit and knelt to try to find the blasted thing.

Suddenly Vic was there. "What's the matter? Are you all right?"

Was he really worried?

"Damn wooden deck," she muttered. "I've got a splinter in my foot."

"Is that all? The way you screamed, I thought you were really hurt."

Now he sounded irritated, as if her wound wasn't worth his attention.

"I am," she told him. "This feels like a wooden spike in my foot."

"What do you expect when you go around barefoot?"

"You were walking barefoot this morning."

"I can do it. My soles are hardened." He took her foot in his hand; Eve clutched his shoulder to steady herself. "Your foot's too delicate. The skin's soft." As his hand moved caressingly along the sole of her foot, she giggled. He looked up at her. "I thought it hurt."

"It hurts like the dickens." So maybe she was exaggerating a wee bit.

"Then why're you giggling?"

"You're tickling me."

On the verge of laughter himself, Vic shook his head. "You are something else."

"I know," she said apologetically. "Can you get it out?"

"Not here. I can't see. We'll have to get some light on it." He stood, taking her arm to lead her to his boat. As she stepped down, Eve winced in pain. Vic scooped her up in his arms.

"You don't have to carry me. I can walk."

Gruffly, Vic said, "You'll just drive that thing in deeper or pick up another splinter."

Eve was glad he ignored her halfhearted protest. It was nice being cradled in his arms this way. As he stepped onto the *Hippolyta*, she felt her robe parting. Remembering that she had nothing on underneath, she clutched it desperately. His knowing glance told her Vic had guessed why she was doing that, but he made no comment. Most men would have been prompted to say something flirtatious or sexually suggestive. Was he different, or not interested?

Too soon her little ride ended when Vic deposited her on a deck chair. He brought out a first-aid kit and large flashlight and sat on the deck, pulling her foot onto his lap.

"Ah, there it is. You're right," he said. "It's pretty big."

"I told you."

Vic took out a pocket knife and flipped open a thin blade.

"Hold on there. What's the knife for? I haven't signed any consent form for surgery."

"Relax. I'm just going to ease the skin away a little. Then I can take the splinter out with tweezers."

"Oh, goodie. I haven't played doctor in years."

He rewarded her joking comment with a slight smile.

"Go to it," she told him.

"Spunky, aren't you?" He bent to his task. "I'll try not to hurt you."

It did hurt some, but Vic was deft and gentle at the same time.

"Here's the culprit," he exclaimed, holding up a sliver of wood on his pincers.

"Let me have it."

He handed it to her. Puzzled, he asked, "You intend to keep it?"

"Why not? I've heard some people keep their gallstones."

He let out a belly laugh.

Eve grinned. "That's a sound I like. You should do that often."

"Stay put," he commanded, and disappeared to return with iodine and a Band-Aid. "Just in case," he said, smearing the puncture with iodine and covering it with the bandage. "All done."

"Too bad. I was enjoying this part." An understatement by far, but should she be telling him so?

He stood. "Ready to go back?"

"If I must." Eve made no objection when he lifted her again into his arms. Why risk another splinter? She let her arms circle his neck and ventured to touch the dark hair curling there. As he took a long step onto the *Six Pack*, her robe fell away somewhat, allowing a glimpse of silken thighs. As Vic set her gently down, Eve felt a tremor go through him. Keeping her arms around his neck, she made no move to step away. She shivered slightly.

"Are you cold?" His voice was a gruff whisper.

"A little." But her trembling had nothing to do with the outside temperature.

Vic smoothed tendrils of hair back from her forehead. "Your hair's wet."

"I . . . I just washed it."

He was running his hands through her hair, rubbing her scalp, then touching her delicate ears, his caressing fingertips sending shock waves coursing through her, waves which converged someplace in the center of her being and made her melt against him.

Then Vic brought his mouth to hers in a gentle, lingering kiss that was an agony of sweetness. The sweetness soon turned into fire; Eve's lips parted to allow her flaming tongue to taste his lips. With a muffled groan, Vic crushed her to him painfully, but it was a pain she welcomed in her desire to get close to him, to crawl inside him if she could. His tongue spoke desire, darting into her mouth, seeking her sweetness. He kissed her eyes and face and neck, tracing, tasting, nibbling, and arousing every sensitive nerve. When he brought his lips to the cavity between her breasts, her robe fell away to expose one ivory, pink-tipped mound. Like a magnet, it attracted his roving lips. Vic teased the tip erect then moved to the other side to continue his magic.

Vic raised his head to take her mouth again and Eve softened against him. Her desire, pliant and passionate, inflamed him. It was neither submissive nor strident, and more seductive than anything he'd experienced. With Maria . . . Guiltily, he left the thought unfinished. He felt Eve's trembling and the fiery invitation in her lips. If he didn't stop now . . .

Vic pulled back and gripped her arms hard. It was painful to see the glow in her eyes replaced by surprise and confusion. He shook his head to free it from the haze of passion. "I'm sorry," he said.

"Why?"

"For taking advantage of the situation." He smiled and tried for a light tone. "That's not my usual style."

"Who's complaining?" she said shakily. "It wouldn't have happened if I hadn't wanted it to."

He pulled her robe tightly about her. "You just don't know what's good for you."

"And you do?" she challenged. "Vic, I'm a grown woman."

How much of a woman he was just beginning to fathom. With difficulty, he resisted the urge to take her in his arms again. *Keep it light*, he told himself.

"A woman who drops keys overboard and gets splinters in her feet," he said.

"Make that singular. One key . . . one splinter . . . one foot."

"I stand corrected. But you do seem to be accident prone."

She arched her brows and gave him a mischievous grin. "Are you calling yourself an accident?"

"Be serious."

"Are you sure you want me to be?" She was being deliberately provocative.

"Yes . . . I mean no." He shook his head with frustration. "Hell, I don't know what I mean." Eve was confusing him.

"Don't yell," she cautioned in a hushed voice. "The neighbors . . ."

"I wasn't yelling. And what neighbors?"

She pointed. There was a gull perched on one of the pilings to which the *Six Pack* was tied. "I don't think he's eavesdropping," Vic said dryly.

Eve tilted her head. "Can you tell if a seagull's a he or a she?"

"No, I can't tell," he said with exasperation. "And what has that got to do with anything? Do you always come up with these non sequiturs?"

"Only at moments of heightened emotional tension," she said with soft amusement.

He groaned, pulled her to him, thought better of it, gave her a peck on the forehead, and said, "I think you'd better go in."

"Do I have to?"

Vic hesitated, summoned his willpower, then said, "Yes." Obediently, she did.

Later, lying in bed, Eve relived all the luscious sensations Vic had aroused. She felt more alive than she had in years. Maybe she would save that sliver of wood; it had started something new and wonderful for her. Why had Vic held back like that? Protecting her from herself? She'd show him how wrong he was. She didn't need protection. She needed love.

Just before she fell asleep, she heard the sharp clack of thunder. He'd been right about the rain clouds, though.

Vic was in no hurry to get out of bed. He opened his eyes, but the usual galvanizing response of his body failed to follow. He stretched lethargically and frowned, annoyed at himself. This wasn't like him. True, he hadn't slept much, but that wasn't it. Even with only four or five hours sleep, it was his custom to awaken early, get right out of bed, and be up and about.

Up and about . . . what?

Come on, he told himself. There was plenty to do—that report he hadn't finished reading last night, the notes to prepare for the managers' meeting in Atlanta tomorrow. Now that he had the necessary financing, he should be planning for the new warehouses in Georgia and the Carolinas. He should . . .

But his mind bounced off these considerations, so filled with thoughts of last night—and of Eve.

She'd gotten to him. Boy, had she ever! So sweet. He'd had to force himself to pull away. He closed his eyes, remembering the aching desire she'd aroused in him. Why had he stopped himself?

Maria?

Perhaps, at least partially, despite the "no strings" understanding he and Maria had. Traveling as much as they each did, separated for long periods, they'd both indulged in transitory liaisons. Nothing serious.

But why make something *serious* out of this attraction to a small-town teacher on summer vacation? So she had a special kind of appeal . . . and Al Fraser had asked him to watch out for his new tenant. Given the proximity of the two boats, keeping an eye on Eve would be easy—keeping his hands off her was the problem. Last night her ardor had seemed to match his. Perhaps all she wanted from him was to add a little zest to her New York holiday. That he could provide.

What he didn't want was any long-term entanglement or emotional bind. He liked his life just as it was. He'd brought the business along to where he could take time off when he wanted, to sail, race the *Hippolyta*, relax. Maybe, after the Atlanta trip, he'd take off for NewPort or Block Island, spend a week sailing, swimming, and just lazing around.

Alone?

Maria might be free. He didn't bother trying to keep track of her hectic tennis schedule. But she'd never last a whole week on the *Hippolyta*. Maria liked the excitement and competition of a race or the fun of a party on the boat, but that was it. After a few hours aboard, she went stir crazy. "What I need's a boat the size of a tennis court," she'd joked.

Now Eve Marsden on the other hand . . . Really out of her element here at the marina, yet so determined to take hold. But it wasn't her pluckiness which sent this surge of heat through him now. Last night . . . her lips so sweet and full of promise, the clinging warmth of her body. Another minute and he could have slipped that robe from her shoulders and—

Vic groaned aloud and heaved himself upright. Time for a shower.

FOUR

Eve literally fell out of bed. Her alarmed yelp coincided with the thud that rocked the *Six Pack*. She lay tangled in her top sheet in the small space between her dinette table/bed and the galley part of the cabin. There was another thud, someone jumping onto the deck. Then Vic calling, "Eve . . . you okay?"

For a second, she hadn't known where she was. His voice made her remember and she smiled.

Vic rattled the knob on the cabin door, then opened it. He took one step down, leaning into the cabin. "What the hell . . . ?"

Eve pushed up on her elbows and looked up at him. "I guess I had a rude awakening this morning."

"I can see that. Are you all right?"

He came the rest of the way down, bent over, and lifted her up. The sheet fell away. Eve clutched his arms to steady herself. "I'm fine." She gave a short laugh. "You could say I woke up with a bang."

Vic's frowning concern eased into a smile. He was bare-chested, wearing only faded denim shorts. It was sinful, how good he looked so early in the morning, freshly shaved and shining, even his hair combed. And here she

50

was, still disheveled and puffy from sleep, and wearing these decidedly unsexy cotton shorty pajamas.

Vic stepped away and looked her over. "No broken bones or you wouldn't be joking about it." He picked up the sheet and tossed it on the bed. "These close quarters take some getting used to. Actually, this is supposed to be a double bed."

"Cozy."

"Makes for real togetherness," he said with a suggestive half-smile.

She smiled back. "Nothing wrong with that."

He hesitated, then turned to go. With one foot on the lower step, he swerved. "Why the hell didn't you lock this door?"

His sudden gruffness startled her. "I guess I forgot."

"Well, don't," he ordered. "This is Manhattan, not some safe little suburb."

"I thought, with you right here . . ." Flustered by his sudden change of mood, Eve stumbled on her words.

"Just lock this door from now on, okay?"

"Okay."

Vic ducked under the door hatch and disappeared.

Eve gave an explosive sigh, then started to dismantle her bed.

Eve touched the deepening black-and-blue mark on her left hip tenderly and winced. It was going to be a doozie. All these little mishaps . . . Vic probably had her pegged as a real klutz. But she'd learn. She'd show him.

Ten minutes later, wearing a flared sundress of brightly patterned Mexican cotton, she stepped out on deck. It was a bright and breezy morning, a feel-good kind of morning. Eve had a pot of coffee going and pancake batter mixed and ready. She would invite Vic to breakfast.

She recognized the sound as the startup of a motor, but didn't realize it was the *Hippolyta* until she saw Vic loosening the lines from his cleats. She stepped onto the dock.

"'You're going out?" she called, trying to keep the disappointment out of her voice.

"Yeah. Rain's over and the wind's just right this morning." Again his mood had changed. Now brisk and cheery, he added, "Can't pass it up."

Trying not to make her invitation sound like an appeal, Eve said, "Why not wait till after breakfast? I'm making pancakes."

"Thanks, but I had breakfast before you fell out of bed." He grinned at her. "And this wind won't last long." He stepped deftly onto the dock and loosened the two stern lines. He wrapped one around the right pole, then handed her the looped end. "Toss this onto the boat when I tell you. Can you do that?"

"Of course." What did he think, that she'd hurl it into the water or something? Serve him right if she did. But why was she annoyed with him? The man had a perfect right to go for a morning sail, even if he left her with too much pancake batter and a let-down feeling.

"Now," he yelled, and she unwound the line and tossed it into the cockpit. "Good girl," he said, and waved goodbye. Eve watched as he maneuvered out of the slip and headed away from the congested marina area into the river. She had always loved seeing the grace of a sailboat cutting through the water—from a distance. But this time, she wished she were aboard with Vic. Eve stood and watched until she lost sight of the *Hippolyta*.

Eve went back to the *Six Pack*, poured herself some coffee, and sat on deck. There were so many things she could do today. This was Manhattan, with all its exciting attractions—the galleries, museums, theaters, the streets of Greenwich Village, and the shops of Fifth Avenue. So why was she sitting here yearning after a sailboat with the unnautical name of *Hippolyta*?

"Yoo hoo."

The call interrupted Eve's reverie. *Yoo hoo?* No one said that anymore. Except someone like the portly figure coming down the dock toward her, a woman in an old-fashioned housedress who looked like a character out of a '30s movie. Reaching the *Six Pack*, the woman smiled cheerfully and introduced herself.

"Hello," she said. "I'm Loretta Stubblefield. Funny name, but people remember it. My mother's responsible for the Loretta part. Guess she hoped I'd be delicate and wispy like Loretta Young. My husband, Hal, now he made me into a Stubblefield. Mind if I come aboard?"

Without waiting for an answer, Loretta Stubblefield hiked up her skirt and, with a nimbleness that surprised Eve, hopped over and into the cockpit. She had a round face, gray-streaked brown hair gathered into a bun, and wire-rimmed spectacles on her nose. "Is that coffee? Got any extra? Haven't had mine yet. I'm parked down there." She pointed. "As near the facilities as I can get so I don't have to walk far. Mine's the *Someday*."

"Pardon?"

"The name of my boat, *Someday*."

"Oh. That's an interesting name."

"Hal picked it. Because of all the plans we had, like cruisin' down to Florida and the Caribbean. Maybe even around the world. Some day. Then he went and died a week after we got the boat."

"That's terrible."

"Yeah. But that was fourteen years ago. So now I cruise without him." It was a matter-of-fact statement. Loretta wasn't looking for sympathy. Eve knew how she felt.

The boat on the end was at least a forty-two-foot cabin cruiser. "You go out alone?" Eve asked.

"Who goes out?" Loretta grinned. "I just do like we always used to, Hal and me, sit with the magazines and charts and plan where to go. Like Vic says, I cruise with my imagination. Saves me a lot of gas money," she added with a grin. "Now, where's that coffee?"

"How about some pancakes to go with it? I've got the batter all ready."

Loretta was easily persuaded. When she'd finished her sixth and last pancake, she gave a contented sigh and put down her fork. "Delicious," she said. "Lucky for me your company didn't show."

"Company?" Eve pretended surprise.

"You trying to tell me you'd've eaten all those pancakes by yourself?"

"No." With a bland, innocent expression, Eve said, "Actually, I thought I'd ask Vic over. He's been so helpful."

"Right neighborly idea," said Loretta with a knowing grin. "But he took off, did he?"

"The wind . . . perfect for a morning sail."

"Sure. Independent cuss, that one."

Eve averted her gaze. "So I gathered."

Had there been something wistful in her voice that made Loretta's look turn curious? Eve quickly steered the conversation in another direction, asking questions about life at the marina. Loretta had a wealth of stories to tell. Eve poured them the last of the coffee and they went outside to sit on the deck. Loretta noticed Eve was distracted whenever she heard a moving boat. "Vic'll be back soon," she said.

"I wasn't . . ." Eve paused, forgoing a flimsy denial, then asked, "How d'you know?"

Loretta licked a forefinger and held it up. "Wind's gone. He'll be coming in."

Resuming her descriptions of the vicissitudes of living aboard a boat, Loretta launched into a vivid account of the snowstorm two winters ago when the power on the West Side had gone out.

"But Vic got this generator, and about ten of us crowded onto his boat until it was all over. We were sleeping every which way, trippin' over each other." Loretta laughed at the memory. "But it was fun. Vic'd make a food run and come back with pizza or Chinese, and we'd have a party. Maria thought he was nuts since he didn't have to stay here. He's got that apartment on the East Side, you know."

"I thought Vic lived here on his boat."

"He does, mostly. Says the other place is convenient for business entertaining. Maria, she uses it when she's in town."

Pretending casual interest, Eve asked, "A business associate?"

Loretta's attention was distracted. She stood up and pointed. "See, I told you. Here he comes."

She waved. Vic, at the wheel, saw them and waved back. Eve followed Loretta onto the dock where they waited as Vic turned the *Hippolyta* and backed into his slip. A few feet away, he cut the motor and came astern to pick up a line. Loretta reached as he threw and caught it easily. Vic picked up another line, glanced at Eve, then threw it. She reached out, grabbed, almost lost it as the boat swung away, but held on. "Gently," Vic cautioned as the women pulled the boat closer. "Okay—hold her there," he said, and went forward to fix the bow lines. Loretta wound her line around a deck cleat. Noticing Eve's intent observation, Loretta undid her knot and then, slowly, exaggerating the maneuver, fastened her line again. Eve bent and did the same thing.

"Good," Vic said.

Eve looked up from her squatting position to see him leaning over the stern. Faint praise, but she loved it. Now to get up without falling back on her butt. She managed.

"You missed a great breakfast, big fella," Loretta told him. "Banana pancakes . . . delicious. Your loss was my gain. Probably a two-pound gain," she added ruefully, patting her ample hips. "Well, I best be moseying along."

They watched her waddling gait as Loretta made her way down the dock.

"She's a pretty terrific lady," Vic said. "When I first

met Loretta, I wondered what she was doing here. She didn't seem to fit.''

''Like me?'' Eve didn't wait for a reply. ''First impressions can be deceiving.''

Vic grinned. ''I'm willing to change mine. You're learning,'' he conceded. ''I'm beginning to think you'll survive the summer.''

''Thanks.'' A deliberate reminder that her time here, her time with him, was temporary? That *was* true, but right now she was interested in beginnings, not endings.

''How was your sail?'' she asked.

''Too short.''

''Maybe the wind will pick up and you can go out again.''

He looked at his watch. Sunlight burnished the hair that curled around his watch strap. Her eyes strayed to his bare chest, the tendrils there glinting with a darker glow. It was hot now with the breeze gone, and a slight sheen covered his skin. Eve was tempted to slide her finger across his chest and . . .

She quickly averted her glance.

''Not today,'' Vic said. ''Duty calls. No more goofing off. I've got to get to my office.''

''Oh. That's too bad.''

''Is it?''

His narrow-eyed look was disconcerting.

''Why?'' he asked.

He had this knack for flustering her with a glance or a word. ''Well . . . it's such a nice day,'' she answered.

''You have something special in mind for this nice day?''

Something special in mind, something Vic could share? She wished she could say she had. But if he was busy, why was he asking? The man thoroughly confused her. ''I haven't decided yet,'' she replied.

He hesitated, then said, ''Maybe, another day, we can do something together.''

"That would be nice." An understatement, given the excited anticipation that surged through her.

"When I get back from Atlanta," he added.

Her anticipation froze. "You're going away?"

"Tomorrow. That's why I have all this get-ready work to do."

Did he say it regretfully, or was she projecting her own disappointment on to him?

"Will you be gone long?" Just a neighborly question.

"Probably not."

Apparently he wasn't going to be any more definite than that. Eve didn't pursue it. After all, Victor Adesso didn't have to report his comings and goings to her.

"I'd better get cleaned up and on my way," he said.

"Sure. See you," she said with a jaunty wave and returned to the *Six Pack*.

It turned out to be a good day for Eve after all. On a whim, she headed downtown for the South Street Seaport, a part of New York she'd never explored. On her rare trips to New York with Graham, the attractions had always been museums and concerts, indoor activities. Graham hadn't been interested in things nautical. But then, neither had she—until now.

Eve took the midday walking tour of the ships and piers. Most visitors were in groups or twosomes. Though she'd gotten used to solitary pleasures these last few years, certain experiences, like this one, would be more fun with a companion. Vic Adesso kept cropping up in her thoughts.

Her tour took her on board the *Ambrose* lightship and the four-masted bark *Peking*, where she was fascinated by photographs made during old-time Cape Horn passages. Too bad Vic wasn't here. He'd probably love looking at the pictures showing the life of canvas seamen on trading vessels in the early 1900's.

Her late lunch was a dozen clams from a bar in a little fish house on the corner of Fulton Street, a great little place that she'd have to tell Vic about. Eve's afternoon ended with a Bluegrass concert on Pier 16. Did Vic like Bluegrass? she wondered.

Walking back to the Fulton Street parking lot to get her car, Eve realized that this whole experience was tinged with thoughts of Vic Adesso, that he'd been very much on her mind all day, probably why she chose to come down here in the first place. His influence was there even when he was not. And they'd known each other such a short time.

Nothing like this had ever happened to her before. It was exciting, but scary, too. Eve was meeting the challenge of living on a boat. The challenge offered by Vic Adesso was something else.

After stopping at Caruso's for a few provisions, Eve got back to the marina a little before six. Loretta hailed her as she got out of her car.

"Eve, yoo-hoo. Over here."

The voice came from the small grassy picnic area to the side of the parking lot. Eve had noticed a couple of people using the charcoal grills yesterday. This evening Loretta was the only one. With a barbecue fork, Loretta gestured for Eve to join her.

"Bo got the steaks, and there's salad and corn," Loretta said. "I'm doin' the cooking, and if you've got something to contribute, you can eat with us. Or even if you don't." Loretta noticed where Eve's glance went. "He's not back yet," she volunteered.

Eve didn't bother to deny the inference that she was looking for Vic. On the grill, three large T-bones were sizzling. "Smells good. Are you sure there's enough?"

"Plenty. Bo gets them from Caruso's for free, kind of a perk for bein' the go-between on phone orders. There's another steak in the cooler, just in case we get a hungry latecomer," she added with a smile.

"Okay, then," Eve agreed. She dug into her grocery bag. "I've got two kinds of melon and Dutch apple pie."

"A feast," Loretta declared as Bo ambled over to join them. "Bo, tonight we eat like kings."

"Allus do when you cook, Loretta," Bo said, doffing his stained fisherman's hat in a courtly gesture. His forehead, moist with sweat, was indented with a ring from the pressure of the headband. "Allus do."

They were halfway through eating when the Jaguar pulled into the parking lot. Vic appeared not to see them as he headed straight for the pier. Loretta's "Yoo-hoo" stopped him. He turned and waved.

"Come eat with us," Loretta called.

Vic came only part way. "Thanks, but I had something at the office."

"So have something more," Loretta said.

"C'mon," Bo said. "Steak's real good."

"And there's melon and pie for dessert," Eve added.

Vic looked at Eve. "You're tempting me."

"I'm trying." *But you're being very elusive*, she thought to herself.

He hesitated, then shook his head. He gestured with his arms and the heavy attaché case he clutched in one hand grazed the dirt, but Vic didn't notice, or didn't care. He'd rolled up his shirtsleeves and loosened his collar and tie. He looked frustrated and weary. "Thanks, but I can't. Today was a real foul-up. Nothing went right. I've got a mountain of paperwork to go through before morning."

His voice matched his tired appearance. Eve thought of telling him he needed to relax, but would she sound like a mother hen? All she said was, "That's too bad."

"It happens." He shrugged and started to walk off. Over his shoulder, he called, "Enjoy."

But Eve's pleasure had diminished.

A corner of Vic's cabin on the *Hippolyta* housed his office space. He'd often claimed the tight quarters were an advantage. Desk, computer, printer, files—all within arm's reach. Everything immediately accessible.

So why the hell couldn't he find the signed copy of the lease agreement for that property in Charlotte? That was only one of the problems that had cropped up today, Jamison's sudden change of heart and trying to renege on his contract. Probably angling for a better deal. But Vic knew the offer he'd made the man was a fair one.

Where could he have put that lease? He'd already looked in this file cabinet, but he gave it another try. No luck! He slammed it shut, and sat on the edge of the desk. What now? Vic bent his head back, trying to stretch away the tension.

He heard footsteps on the dock and through his window saw Eve coming back to the *Six Pack* carrying a grocery bag. The little dinner party must be over. He'd been tempted to join them and put work off until later, but giving in to temptation wasn't his custom. Self-discipline was. Being in complete control of his life was important to him.

Could Eve Marsdon turn out to be a threat to that control?

He watched as Eve swung the *Six Pack* close and boarded, managing easily now. That slim, lithe figure, so much eagerness and warmth—a threat? Not likely. She disappeared below. Vic turned back to his desk.

Now where else could he look for that damn lease?

It had to be at the office or . . . Wait a minute—the apartment! Mostly Vic lived here on the *Hippolyta*, but he maintained a condo on the East Side of Manhattan as a business convenience. He'd stopped off there for a quick change after getting back from Raleigh a week ago. He wasn't sure, but he might have laid it down on the bed or a table. If Maria were there, she could look for it. Maybe she was. He could never keep track of that crazy schedule of hers. He dialed and waited, hoping the answering machine wouldn't kick in. It didn't. With relief, Vic heard Maria's throaty "Hello."

"Maria?"

"Who else?" She laughed. "You haven't been distributing keys to other females, have you, Vic?"

"No. When did you get in? How long are you staying?"

"How about a 'How are you? How was Australia?' "

He complied. "How are you? How was Australia?"

"I'm tired. Australia was awful. I didn't even make the semifinals."

So that was it. "I'm sorry."

"Not as much as I am," she said wearily.

Losing always put Maria in a bad mood, but she sounded worse than usual. "It's not the end of the world."

"I don't know about that." Her laugh was humorless. "Australia sure seemed like the end of something. Look, why don't you come over?"

"Can't," Vic said apologetically. "I'm up to my ears in paperwork."

"Do it tomorrow."

"I'm going to Atlanta in the morning. That's why I'm calling."

"Your logic escapes me," Maria scoffed. "You didn't know I was here, and you're calling because you're going to Atlanta tomorrow? Vic, are you on something?"

"No." Vic explained about the missing papers. Maria went to look and reported that she'd found a manila folder on the dresser. "I'll bring it to you," she offered. Vic protested, but Maria told him, "You're busy and I'm not. I'll be there in a jif. Bye."

Vic was surprised. Not that Maria meant to be inconsiderate, but obsession with her tennis career made for tunnel vision, often closing out her awareness of other people's needs. He wondered if she had something on her mind. Well, he'd find out soon enough.

He spent the next fifteen minutes refiguring cost estimates on a computer spreadsheet. While he was printing out the hard copies, he went out on deck for some air. It was after eight and the sun was almost down behind the

Jersey skyline. The apartment he owned overlooked Central Park, but nothing could beat this view. A passing ferry boat tooted, temporarily drowning out the distant sounds of traffic on the Henry Hudson Parkway. This was one of his favorite times of the day at the marina. Eve should be out here enjoying it.

At that very moment she appeared, the top half of her emerging from the cabin. A breeze turned her short black hair into a dancing aureole. She wore a pink T-shirt, the front of which was emblazoned with a gaudily painted parrot, its head comfortably cushioned on her breast.

"Hi," he said. "I was just thinking about you."

She smiled. "How's that for mental telepathy? Me, too. I mean I was coming up to ask if you wanted a cup of coffee. I'm about to make some."

Reluctantly, he declined. "No thanks. I've still got a ton of paperwork inside."

"Do you get a feeling of déjà vu about this conversation?" Eve asked with a sparkly laugh. "It seems I'm always offering you coffee and you're always saying no. Is this a trend or something?"

He shook his head. "I hope not."

"You don't have to take a long break. I can bring it over to you."

He liked her coaxing tone, but this wasn't the time. "I'd better pass. How about a rain check?"

"Okay then. When you come back."

"Thursday. I'll be back Thursday."

Now why had he said that? He didn't have a definite return for the day after tomorrow. Vic liked to allow for unexpected developments that might require his attention. But he *could* finish up in Atlanta by Thursday if he wanted to. And he suddenly wanted to.

"So we have a coffee date for Thursday," Eve said, then suddenly remembered, "Oh, that's the night of Glen Rader's party."

"So it is. I gather you've met Mr. Rader."

"Briefly."

"He make a pass?"

She laughed. "He hinted."

"Really?" Vic frowned. "Subtlety's usually not Glen's style. Watch out for that guy."

"I can handle his type."

Vic wasn't so sure. Glen had the reputation of being a ladies' man who flirted with every attractive woman. Not to be taken seriously, according to Maria, who got a kick out of him, but charming and harmless. Vic didn't agree with the harmless part. Not after that episode with Sharon two years ago.

Sharon Rosen had worked in Vic's office, a sweet girl from upstate New York who was engaged to a young accountant. Dazzled by Rader's attentions and believing his promises, Sharon had broken her engagement and quit her job to cruise down to Florida with Glen. After the cruise, Glen dumped her, and the disillusioned girl had gone back home to Cobbleskill. Sharon had been naive, but even sophisticated women fell for Rader's line. Vic wanted to believe that Eve was immune, but the man was not to be trusted.

"You're going to Glen's party, aren't you?" Eve asked.

"Yes." It was a sudden decision. "We can go over together. After coffee," he added with a smile.

"Sounds good to me."

There was a sweet sincerity in her voice and her smile—so very appealing.

Eve started back down, hesitated, then asked, "Was there something on your mind? I mean, what you said just before . . . that you were thinking of me?"

"I was wondering why you weren't out enjoying this sunset." Vic made an expansive gesture toward the sky. "It's one of the perks you get for living here."

Eve came all the way up, pushed aside a cushion, and climbed onto the bench across the stern to look all around. The sun was behind her darkly silhouetted figure. Her slender body stretched gracefully in a watchful pose. For a second, both were completely still. Vic gazed admiringly at the picture she presented, narrowed his eyes, and saw another picture: himself at her side, their arms about each other. He resisted the impulse to make that picture real.

"It is beautiful," Eve said softly.

It became suddenly quieter. His printer had stopped. Vic shook off the momentary spell. "I'd better get back to work," he said.

Eve leaped from the seat. "If you change your mind about coffee, just come over," she told him.

"I'll wait till Thursday," he said, and went below.

Eve fixed herself a cup of instant. No sense brewing a whole pot. She'd have it on deck. Alone. Some music would be nice. She took her little portable radio up with her—with the headphones so she wouldn't disturb Vic's work. Eve sat facing the river, her back to the dock. Darkness came quickly now. It was as though the sun's setting created a void which night rushed in to fill. Eve sipped her coffee as she listened to the sweetly plaintive music of Manuel DeFalla on her favorite public station.

Her thoughts turned to Vic and their conversation just now. It was clear he didn't trust Glen Rader. Was he being protective? That wasn't the feeling Eve wanted to arouse. After all, she'd been on her own since Graham's death, and was perfectly capable of managing her life. By choice she'd avoided any emotional or sexual involvement. For Eve, the two were inseparable.

And by choice, when she was ready, she would change.

Perhaps her coming to New York, to this particular place, was a turning point, a signal that it was time to start a new phase in her life. Eve's capacity for love had not died with Graham. She'd held it dormant—until now.

Eve didn't hear, but rather sensed someone approaching, a heavy-footed step on the dock. Removing her earphones, Eve turned and saw the woman striding toward her—tall, broad-shouldered, straight blond hair, sleekly muscled legs in white canvas shoes. The kind of woman, Eve thought, who'd reach for the gold cup and claim it as hers, the kind who knew exactly what she wanted. Eve was surprised when the woman stopped at the *Hippolyta*. She spanned the distance from the boat with one long leg, then, with practiced skill, shifted her weight and stepped aboard. "Vic," she called, "I'm here."

To herself, Eve whispered the name that Vic called out—"Maria."

So that was why Vic was so busy tonight.

Maria disappeared into the cabin—where Vic waited.

Eve's peaceful mood was swept away by a tangle of conflicting feelings—jealousy, sadness, resentment, anger at herself, at Vic . . . The Rosarios had hinted that Vic wasn't free. She'd sensed that he was attracted to her, but held himself in check. Was Maria the reason?

Eve turned up the sound of the music, shutting out the muffled voices from Vic's cabin. The dark night now seemed inhospitable and cold. Eve shivered and went below.

_____ FIVE _____

The early-morning shower felt good, clearing away Eve's grogginess. It was barely light when she'd gone into the bathhouse, but now the sky was turning pearly pink. She stopped for a moment, breathing deeply, ingesting the air's freshness. A gravelly sound came from the parking area. There was Vic, putting a suitcase into the back of his car. He saw her and came over.

"Good morning." He flashed a broad smile. "You're up early."

"So're you."

"I have a plane to catch."

His cheerfulness was irritating. "Don't let me keep you."

Vic cocked his head. "Something wrong?"

Her reply came quickly. "No. What could be wrong?" Eve became annoyed at herself for acting this way. She forced a slight smile. "I didn't sleep much last night. Makes me kinda grumpy."

"Did I disturb you?"

Now what kind of question was that?

"I mean with my clattering equipment," he added.

"Oh. No, not at all."

"Because I make it a rule to cease and desist by ten. In fact, last night I stopped much earlier."

As Eve well knew. "You didn't disturb me." Not quite true, but how could she admit it wasn't noise, but the lack of it that had kept her wakeful? Would he mention his visitor? He probably thought it was none of Eve's business. And he was right.

"You're still settling in . . ." he said. "Nervous maybe. It'll pass."

Oh, yeah? Aloud, she said, "I hope you got all your work done."

"No problem. A friend brought some papers I'd misplaced. After that, clear sailing."

"How nice."

He missed the irony. She saw him glance at his watch. "You'd better be on your way or you'll miss your plane."

"Right. See you soon."

"Sure."

Eve walked toward the pier. She'd be damned if she was going to stand there in her bathrobe, waiting to wave as he drove off into the sunset. *Sunrise*, she amended as she saw dawning colors drape over the sky.

Eve walked back slowly, displeased with her performance back there. Because it was a performance. Why couldn't people be completely honest about what they were thinking and feeling? Her words hadn't reflected the thoughts and questions swirling around her head. *The woman who came last night, is she a friend? More than a friend? A lover? Did you make love while I lay in bed wondering?* But she couldn't ask those questions. She had no right.

Eve had gone below at nine-thirty and drawn the curtains of the cabin, determined not to monitor what was going on next door. Resolutely, she'd thumbed through a whole issue of *The National Geographic*, retaining nothing of what she was reading. She couldn't summon any interest in the life cycle of woolly aphids. She'd put the magazine away and gone to bed.

But sleep had been long in coming. A couple of times, voices outside made her raise the curtain to peek, but it was always someone at the other end of the dock. Annoyed with herself, she'd stopped checking. She had tried to lie still. If she thrashed about, she might fall out of bed again. Then maybe Vic would rush over. Or Vic and his companion? Eechgh! Eventually, the *Six Pack*'s gentle rocking lulled her into dozing.

It was a fitful sleep with periods of vague awareness of voices and once, a heavy footfall on the dock, but she'd willfully staved off awakening. Until four in the morning, when she could sleep no longer. She'd gone on deck, but the night was unwelcoming, falling on her like a heavy shroud. The *Hippolyta* was quiet, its cabin light darkened. Was Vic asleep? Was he alone?

Returning to bed, Eve lay awake, trying to sort through her disturbing emotions.

There was no denying the strong attraction she felt for Vic Adesso. Was it only physical? Certainly that was a primary component. That virility he exuded, a pungent masculinity that aroused her senses.

Eve knew herself to be a sensuously responsive person. When she played the piano, the touch of the keys was as pleasing as the sound they emitted. Stone sculpting offered all kinds of tactile pleasures where the doing was more important than the finished piece. Even eating . . . Eve relished the texture of food, not just its taste and aroma. Graham used to tease her about her hedonistic appetites— for everything in life. His own pleasures were more subdued. Dear Graham. She'd sometimes curtailed the enthusiasms that he couldn't appreciate. Marriage called for accommodation. All relationships did.

Vic Adesso didn't strike her as a man who made accommodations.

But over a short term, the few weeks she would be here, why did it matter? Vic intrigued her. Beyond the physical thing, there was the challenge he offered and her response to the strength of his personality. He seemed to dare her to vie for his respect. She wanted to meet that challenge.

Even if there were another woman in his life? That stately blonde, like a modern Hippolyta. Did he have Maria in mind when he'd named his boat?

Eve had shaken off the unwelcome thought, gotten out of bed, and gone for a shower.

But talking to Vic just now brought back her confusion. He had called Maria "a friend". Just how broad was his definition of friendship?

Eve had looked forward to this summer sojourn in New York as a change of pace, a chance to revitalize her life. But perhaps she was getting more than she'd bargained for.

As he drove off, Vic wondered about Eve's attitude. Last night she'd been so friendly and warm, but just now, cool and distant. She gave out mixed signals. But then, he probably did, too, since he wasn't sure what he wanted from this woman.

With Maria, he'd had a straightforward understanding from the beginning. They'd spent time together when their schedules coincided, and slept together when their inclinations coincided. Both occurrences were less frequent of late. Maria had never objected to Vic's erratic work schedule or long absences because she lived a similar hectic life, traveling the tennis circuit all over the world. They had some mutual friends, and shared interests in sports, Italian opera, and Oriental cuisine. But there were large areas of their individual lives that were completely separate. And that was fine with both of them.

A tough broad, he'd once jokingly called Maria. She had taken it as a compliment. She lived her own life, not his, and he admired her independence. Vic didn't want to be responsible for anyone else's life and happiness. The macho male was a stereotype he disliked, a perverse way of satisfying masculine ego needs.

But last night, Maria had been different. Almost too polite, and straining to be nice. She'd stayed for quite a while, yet she hadn't come on to him, inviting an intimacy he wouldn't have welcomed. They hadn't spent much time together during the last few months, keeping in touch mostly by telephone. Their divergent schedules, Vic assumed, although he hadn't given it much thought.

Last night Maria had seemed disturbed. After ten years, they knew each other well. Ten years of . . . Vic wasn't sure how to characterize their relationship. An affair? But physical intimacy had lately taken second place, no longer vital to their friendship.

Maria had seemed uneasy, her conversation disjointed. Some of her comments had to do with missing out on things other women enjoyed, like marriage and a family. She wondered how long she could, or should, go on making tennis the main focus of her life.

She'd occasionally talked like this before, perhaps more frequently in the last year or so, but never with any serious intent of quitting the game. Was she serious this time? Then suddenly she'd veered into another subject, mentioning the upcoming tournament in Chicago and how she hoped her luck would change there.

Maria was probably worried about her playing slump, that was all. Vic rationalized that she was in a down mood. A winning match would renew her verve and their easy camaraderie.

She'd asked if he'd mind picking her up this morning so she could drive him to the airport and use the Jaguar while he was gone. He'd said okay. All it meant was leaving a few minutes early. Vic glanced at the dashboard clock. No problem. There was plenty of time, and Maria would be waiting at the front entrance. They'd done this before. She preferred cabs to keeping a car in the city, but liked to borrow the Jag for longer drives and grand entrances. This time, the occasion was some kind of celebrity bash in Long Island.

Maybe the party would cheer her up. Tennis gatherings always had the opposite effect on him. Maria's pro friends talked and talked and talked, but always about the game—the tennis circuit, the last tournament, the next tournament, who played well, who badly. Fact, conjecture, gossip, but all about *the game*.

He thought of Glen Rader's party. Usually his parties were real booze bashes, but at least there'd be a varied group. Glen cultivated a broad range of acquaintances, business associates, media types, boating enthusiasts, and a flock of the glamorous young women he dated. He customarily had a specific favorite in tow.

Eve this time?

Vic didn't like that notion at all. But it wasn't likely, he told himself. They'd only just met, and surely Eve wasn't susceptible to Rader's type of charm. Or was she? Vic reminded himself that he hardly knew Eve Marsdon.

As expected, Maria was waiting. She seemed in a better mood and chattered animatedly on the way to the airport. At the departure terminal, she got out to take the driver's seat and gave him a perfunctory kiss.

"When're you coming back?" she asked.

"Probably Thursday. Will you still be around?"

"Maybe. I'm not sure."

Her uncertainty wasn't unusual. Maria was known to take off on a moment's notice. "No problem," Vic told her. "Just leave the car in the garage like always."

"You got it," she said.

Later, as he checked in, Vic realized he hadn't mentioned Glen's party to Maria. She'd gone with him a couple of times in the past. But she might not even be in town, he rationalized. And missing one of Rader's shindigs was no tragedy.

Except this time, Vic found himself looking forward to Thursday—and the reason was Eve Marsdon.

* * *

After breakfast, Eve hefted her piece of alabaster up to one of the wooden picnic tables on the bank, spread some newspapers, and started to work the stone. There was immense satisfaction in handling her sculpting tools. Therapeutic. Working with her hands always seemed to ease her mind. Much better than sitting around stewing about Vic Adesso. Such a frustrating man! She tried to put him out of her mind as she chipped away with hammer and chisel and used her heaviest rasp to smooth down the rough edges. Before long, she was layered with gritty white dust.

She worked away most of the morning, attracting different audiences for brief periods. Eve met a dozen new people, including more of the regulars, who introduced themselves by the names of their boats. There was a pregnant young woman, pulling a toddler by the hand, who pointed to her boat and said, "We're the *Four Leaf Clover*." Fran and Lou Rosario stopped by and Eve took a break while Fran filled her in on some of the people she'd just met.

There was a conviviality to boat living that reminded Eve of a small town, but with a more diverse and unusual mix of characters. The pregnant girl had sailed solo across the Atlantic four years ago, and the others included a retired judge, an underwater photographer, and a former convict, released last year after serving time for manslaughter. Indeed a motley assortment of people. And of course there was the dapper Glen Rader.

Glen showed up after the others had gone and Eve was alone. She was standing back to study her stone, smoother now with its rough edges gone and contours more defined.

"An artist, too?" Glen said. "My dear, how creative you are." He ran his hands over the alabaster, coming away with dust-covered palms. Frowning, he clapped his hands together, then fanned the particle-laden air from settling on his navy-blue blazer.

"But so messy," he said, coming up to Eve. "You're all sprinkled over." He ran the tip of a manicured finger down her cheek. "As if powdered with sugar. Such a tasty confection."

Eve shook her head, dislodging his touch. "Obviously," she said dryly, "you've never tasted stone dust." She held out a grimy hand, palm up. "Want a lick?"

He threw back his head and laughed. "I think I'll pass, thank you just the same." His smile arched suggestively. "But maybe later, when you're all nice and clean."

"Uh uh. You had your chance."

Glen followed her to the table which held her stone and asked, "What's it going to be?"

"Whatever it wants."

"But what are you making?" he persisted.

"I'm not sure. Whatever comes out of the stone," was her answer.

Eve understood Glen's puzzlement. It had taken her awhile to realize what sculptors meant when they talked about shapes emerging from stone as one worked it. The artist, even one with a preconceived plan of what he hoped to make, had to work within the integral limits of his material. No two stones were alike.

Glen shrugged. He wasn't that interested. "I have a suggestion," he said brightly. "Why not put that . . . ah . . . piece away, change into something frivolous, and go out to dinner with me? I know the most charming little place . . ."

"I'm sorry. I can't."

"Candlelight, music . . . so romantic," he coaxed.

She shook her head. "I really can't."

Glen pouted. "Another date?"

"Dinner with friends." Eve was meeting Greta and George later, so she really wasn't free. Would she have been tempted otherwise? Maybe. What would be the harm?

"Put them off," he persisted.

"I couldn't do that."

"The lady has scruples. How refreshing." Glen assumed a very sad face, asking, "Are you going to keep refusing me like this?"

Eve had to laugh. "I don't know."

"Because I'm devastated. Here I'm being my most utterly charming, and it's not working."

"Glen, just be yourself."

"But my dear, utterly charming *is* myself."

And he gave Eve such an utterly charming smile that she had to laugh again.

"Then you will have dinner with me?" he asked hopefully.

"Not this time."

"Another time then? All right? You can have a rain check."

This rain-checking could get complicated, Eve thought.

Glen leaned over, grazed her mouth with a kiss, then made a show of running his tongue over his lips. "You're right. Very gritty taste." He started off. "Don't forget the party Thursday," he called.

"I won't."

"Two men!" Greta sounded alarmed. From the moment Eve had gotten to the apartment, her friend had plied her with questions. George had tried to intervene.

"Hon, you invited Eve here for dinner, not a third degree," he'd said.

Greta refused to be put off. "Eve, this place sounds like a . . . like a . . . like it's no place for a woman like you."

"What's that supposed to mean, *a woman like me*?"

"Oh, you know. You've been living in a small town. Leonardtown is not like Manhattan."

"No argument there," Eve said. Her friend chose to forget that Eve had spent months in the city years back and had loved it. "But I consider that a plus. Greta, I wanted a change."

"For the worse? What you got is an ordeal."

"You're exaggerating."

Greta ran down the list. "You're living in a cubbyhole that's not even on dry land, you fell out of bed, hurt your foot, dropped the boat keys in the drink, and who knows what else?"

Eve was sorry she'd been so descriptive. Greta was turning funny vignettes into tragic stories. "Minor mishaps," Eve insisted. "And the 'what else' is a great view, marvelous sunsets, and interesting people."

"Aha." Greta pounced. "Like those two guys you described?"

"They're part of it. Greta, what are you so worried about? I can take care of myself. I'm a grown woman. I've been married . . ."

"To a sweet, considerate man who looked out for you. Not like these New York types always on the make." She threw her husband an apologetic look. "Except for you, George."

"Thanks, I think," George said mildly.

"Graham *was* great, and he did look after me." Eve frowned thoughtfully. "I let him because, well, because that's the way it worked for us back then. Graham needed to be protective . . . but when he no longer could be, I discovered that I didn't need protection." Eve paused, then said, "You're right. This is different from Leonardtown, which is fine with me. That's why I came to New York this summer. I *counted* on something different."

"But not dangerous."

"Come on. I'm in no danger."

Greta looked ready to argue the point, but George placed a hand on his wife's arm. "Hey, love, chill out," he cautioned. "You're Eve's friend, not her keeper."

Greta, subdued, looked from one to the other. "I just don't want you to get hurt."

"I know." Eve's smile was affectionate and forgiving. "I won't be."

Now if only she could make that assurance hold.

All the next day, there was no sign of life on the *Hippolyta*. Of course Vic hadn't mentioned any specific time for his return, just that he'd be back on Thursday. Eve spent the morning at housekeeping chores. Or were they properly called *boatkeeping*? Not just the cabin, which took little effort, but sprucing up in the cockpit. Among his boat supplies Al Fraser had chrome polish and a waxing compound for the wooden trim, both of which Eve put to good use.

After lunch, she drove downtown to the New School to check the list of supplies that the art teachers posted for prospective students. Eve already had everything except the three different grades of sandpaper required. At the bulletin board were two other people who were taking the same class—a teenage boy with a partially shaved head and blatantly funky clothes and a silver-haired woman of indeterminate age with dramatic eye makeup and dangling silver earrings. They all introduced themselves and started talking, then walked over to a nearby art supply store together. After making their purchases and picking up cold drinks from a street vendor, they sat for a while in Washington Square Park.

Jason, who lived in California with his mother, was in New York for the court-mandated summer visit with his father, a chef at The Rainbow Room in Rockefeller Center.

"Mom can't cook worth a damn," he said cheerfully. "At least in New York, I eat good."

Reva owned a boutique a couple of blocks away on MacDougal Street. "Come see my shop," she suggested after Jason had taken off.

"My Shop" was actually the name of the store which featured an odd assortment of vintage used clothing along with new imports from India and Asia. A jewelry case was crammed with bangle bracelets and earrings that looked like miniature chandeliers.

"Thirty percent off on anything you like," Reva offered.

Eve never shopped in stores like this. But then, there was no store like this back home. With Reva's encouragement, she tried on a rust-colored sheath-type dress, with black-and-gold embroidery around the neckline and hem.

"Perfect," Reva declared. "It's a short version of a Thai tribal dress. It gives you an exotic look."

"But I'm not the exotic type," Eve said.

"Why be just one type?" the older woman asked. "Be what you want to be. Change your look whenever you want. Here, try these earrings with it."

The earrings, three inches of glittering silvery round discs and chains, were surprisingly light. And they did complete the outfit. Eve surveyed herself in the mirror and nodded at Reva. Why not? She'd wear it to the party tonight.

Glen loved her new look. "My dear, you are amazing," he said, grabbing both her hands in greeting. He'd come down from the boat the minute he saw her approach. "The last time I saw you, you were in grubby clothes layered with dirt. And now—this vision of beauty."

The effusive compliment gave her a needed ego boost. An hour ago, feeling very unpartyish, Eve had considered changing back into old clothes and not coming. Then she'd gotten angry at herself. Just because Vic wasn't here! So he said he'd be back and they'd go to Glen's party together. Well, he didn't make it. No major tragedy. A vague rain check for a cup of coffee didn't constitute an irrevocable date.

Maybe there'd been a glitch in his business dealings, or

his plane was late or something. She had to stop getting upset because Vic didn't fit into her romantic scenario. In fact, she'd better stop creating such a scenario. Vic Adesso was from a different world. They hardly knew each other, really. Except for being temporary neighbors, what did they have in common—aside from the sexual attraction, which Vic was keeping in restraint. It was stupid to sit there and pine. So Eve had picked herself up and had come to join the revelry.

"Why so late?" Glen asked. "I was ready to go looking for you."

"I'm here now," Eve said. The party was in full swing, the guests spilling over onto the dock and a neighboring houseboat. The music from a stereo system was almost drowned out by people noise.

Resplendent in a tentlike flowered muumuu, Loretta called her usual greeting and beckoned with her drink hand. In the other, she held a dish heaped with food. Bo and the Rosarios were with her. Eve waved back, but Glen was steering her away from them onto the boat.

"Come on," he said. "Let's get you something to drink. We're all way ahead of you." A bartender was dispensing drinks in the lounge. There was also a buffet table that a waiter was busy replenishing.

When Eve ordered a glass of white wine, Glen grimaced. "Eve, darling, no."

"What's wrong."

"White wine?" He made a face. "It's so yuppieish. Not at all befitting the way you look."

"What then?"

"Something exotic like a Margarita or a Rusty Nail."

"Rusty Nail?" She laughed, and her long earrings tinkled against her neck. "What an awful name for something that's supposed to be exotic."

"Wait until you taste it. Pure ambrosia—with a kick." He gave the order. "Tim, my man, two Rusty Nails."

While they waited for the drinks, Glen introduced her

to a parade of people who wandered by—semi-celebrities, he called them. "Gareth works with Joe Papp" or "Kimmie does Jane Pauley's hair," went the commentary. When they were out of hearing, Glen would add a gossipy addendum to his introduction. He was unabashedly wicked, and Eve told him so.

"But entertaining, no?" he said as he handed her her drink. He clinked glasses. "To us, and the beginning of a lovely relationship. What's wrong? You don't like my toast?"

"Aren't you getting ahead of yourself?"

"There I go again." Glen heaved an exaggerated sigh. "Moving too fast for you. But dear, sweet Eve, I just cannot help myself."

"Try harder," she said, making him laugh.

Eve changed the toast to "Cheers," and tasted her drink. "Mmm, good. What's in this?"

"Scotch and Drambuie."

"Potent. I better take it slow."

"Not to worry. You're in good hands."

Emphasizing his point, he put his arm around Eve. She didn't pull away. He was harmless, and trying so hard to charm her. Maybe she wasn't experienced at this kind of game, for game it was, but Eve felt perfectly in control.

"Come on," Glen said. "I'll show you *My Weakness*."

A man standing at Glen's elbow overheard and quipped, "Maybe she'd rather see the boat, Glen."

Glen winced and led Eve away. "Crass," he commented. "As if I'd have anything else in mind . . . with all these people around."

The main stateroom had a queen-sized bed and an attached bath. "A real bathtub," Eve marveled. The second stateroom was almost as large. And the galley was a modern, completely equipped kitchen. "You could live aboard in real luxury," Eve commented.

"Only one problem. No Jacuzzi," Glen said plaintively.

They returned to the party crowd on deck. There were

a few people dancing on the dock. "Someone's bound to fall in," Glen said. "Always happens." He kept darting off to see to his guests, but always returned to Eve's side with some new anecdote to relate. His attention was flattering and his conversation entertaining.

He was with Eve and the Rosarios, in the middle of a story, when he interrupted himself to wave at a new arrival. "Ah, there she is," he exclaimed, rushing off to hug a striking blonde and lead her over.

There was something familiar about the woman, her stride, the set of her shoulders . . . Of course. Eve's recognition came in a disturbing flash. Vic's visitor the other night.

"You know Lou and Fran," Glen was saying to Maria. "And this is Eve Marsdon, a newcomer to our happy little group."

The blond woman held out her hand. "I'm Maria Spezia." Her handshake was firm and hearty, her smile dazzlingly white. She wore a pale-blue halter dress revealing broad sun-tanned shoulders. Maria Spezia seemed swathed in an aura of health, strength, and confidence.

Spezia . . . Suddenly Eve recognized the name. And the face, so often featured on the sports pages. "You're the tennis star."

Maria's smile soured a bit. She shrugged. "I don't know about *star*, not lately anyway. The star's been on the wane. Let's just say I'm a tennis *player*."

"You're too modest," Fran protested. "You've been up there with Evert and Billie Jean for years."

"Ten years," Maria said with a rueful smile. "But who's counting? And you'll notice that both those ladies are now retired."

While not an avid fan, Eve liked to watch the big tournament games on television. "You beat Navratilova last year."

Maria laughed. "That was last year. In tennis, last years

don't count." She changed the subject. "Vic says you're leasing Fraser's *Six Pack*."

Glen made a face. "Such a plebeian name!"

"You're a terrible snob," Maria accused, starting a bantering exchange which Lou and Fran also joined. Maria obviously felt at ease with these people, in this surrounding. In Vic's world.

"Where is Vic?" Glen asked.

"Changing out of his power broker suit," Maria replied. "He'll be along."

So they'd come together. From where?

Eve's unasked questions were answered as Maria continued. "I'd borrowed the Jag, so I picked Vic up at Kennedy, ready to chew him out for forgetting to tell me about the party here. Lucky you called me this morning, Glen. But I relented because the poor guy looked beat and said how it had slipped his mind."

"He probably meant to skip my party and keep you all to himself," Glen said. "Not that I blame him. If I had such a lovely, golden goddess . . ." Glen gave a deep sigh.

Maria laughed. "Glen, for the last two years you've been making seductive suggestions. What if I suddenly said yes?"

The question surprised Glen, but he rallied with an answer. "I'd hire a bodyguard to defend me against Vic."

Maria gave her throaty laugh. "Speak of the devil," she said. Vic was coming toward them but was stopped by some people. Maria joined him. The Rosarios drifted away.

"She's quite beautiful," Eve said to Glen.

"Maria? Yes, a real champion. And a good sport," he added with a chuckle. "Vic's a lucky guy."

Maria had put her arm through Vic's.

Eve made her question sound casual. "Have they been going together long?"

"Going together? What a sweet way to put it. Yes,

they've been going together for ages. Quite an item in gossipy sports columns. They've managed to keep everyone guessing for years." Glen chuckled. "They seem to split for a while, go separate ways, and rumors start flying. But they always get back together."

"Do they?" Eve murmured, for want of anything else to say.

Glen glanced over at the other two. "Handsome couple, aren't they? I tease a bit, but Maria's really too tall for me." He placed an index finger under Eve's chin in a gesture she disliked. "Now you, my love, you are just exactly right." He moved his finger caressingly down her neck. Eve backed away.

She looked back at *the handsome couple* and intercepted Vic's gaze. He was staring at her and Glen.

SIX

This was not working out as he'd anticipated, Vic thought as he surveyed the scene. His business in Atlanta had taken longer than he'd thought. The meeting with his managers had gone well, but Jamison had given him a hard time. Not unexpected, but still annoying. It was lucky he'd had the lease with him. They'd finally come to an agreement, but only after hours of haggling. He'd had to take a later flight than planned.

Maria's appearance at the airport had been a surprise. She had phoned his office to find out the flight he was on.

"I figured it'd save time if I picked you up and we drove out together," she had explained. "The party should be rolling by the time we get there."

Apparently Glen Rader had called to tell her to come with or without Vic. Since she was going to be in town until tomorrow, she'd decided why not. He should have guessed Maria would want to go. She found Glen amusing and they got along well.

"Did you forget, or were you going to skip it?" she'd asked.

Evasively, he'd told her, "I wasn't sure when I'd be back."

Actually, until Eve had brought up the subject, he'd had no imperative urge to come. Since then, it was only Eve he'd thought of in connection with tonight.

Driving over tonight, feeling guilty and frustrated by the feeling, he'd told Maria about Eve Marsdon. That is, he'd made casual mention of the young schoolteacher who was renting Al Fraser's boat. Vic had omitted describing the disturbing effect this young schoolteacher was having on him.

"You'll probably meet her tonight," he'd said.

And so it had happened.

The two women had been talking just now when he'd arrived. Glen had introduced them, Maria said, then added, "Glen's really moving in on Eve. See the way he looks at her, like she's some juicy little morsel." Vic glanced over and didn't like what he saw. Rader was practically salivating over Eve.

"I'll go say hello to our lecherous host," he told Maria. "Catch you later."

Glen greeted him jovially. "Vic, my man! Welcome aboard. Glad you could make it."

Eve's "Hello" was pleasant enough. Looking at her, Vic said, "I had to take a later flight than I'd intended."

She nodded, unconcerned.

Vic turned to Glen. "I'd told Eve we'd come over together," he said, for some reason feeling obliged to explain.

"Well, I guess this little lady didn't want to wait for you," said Glen, putting a proprietary hand on Eve's shoulder.

That she tolerated the touch annoyed Vic. He forced a smile. "I think I'll get myself a drink."

"Sure, old man," Glen said. "You know where the bar is."

Eve watched Vic stalk off. He seemed angry. Well, that was just too bad.

Glen had noticed, too. "Our friend's a bit disgruntled. A tiff with Maria, I wonder?"

Eve, suddenly impatient with Glen, was relieved when he was called to greet some boisterous newcomers. The boat deck was now wall-to-wall people. She pushed her way through to the stern and climbed over to the dock to join Bo and Loretta. Bo went off to refill his empty plate.

"See Vic?" Loretta asked.

"Uh huh. He's around." Eve avoided Loretta's inquiring gaze.

"Did you get to meet Maria?"

"Yes."

"And . . . ?"

"And what?"

"What did you think?"

"Loretta, I just met her." Eve shook her head nervously, setting her earrings to tinkling. Why had she worn the noisy things? "She seems very nice."

"Who's nice?" Maria's voice startled Eve. "This is probably the only conversation around where someone isn't getting ripped apart." She came up from behind Eve, holding two dishes of hors d'oeuvres.

"We were talking about you," Loretta told her.

"Really? Well, thank you." Maria flashed her broad smile. "Here," she said, handing a plate to Eve. "I filled one up for you. I figured you hadn't had a chance to sample the goodies."

Eve hadn't been thinking about food. "I haven't. How did you know?"

"With Glen, a gal's got to keep at least one hand free to fend him off," was Maria's laughing reply.

Bo returned. When Loretta looked askance at his heaping plate, he said sheepishly, "Well, it's good grub."

"Bo, you'd call pheasant under glass good grub," Maria teased.

"Nah. I don't even like that stuff."

"Come on, Bo," Loretta said. "You'll eat anything if you're hungry, which is most of the time."

About to pop a shrimp toast into her mouth, Maria started to laugh. "Remember when I made that disastrous lasagna, and Bo was the only one who'd eat it."

It was obvious to Eve that these three liked one another. Their teasing lacked the nasty bite of Glen Rader's.

"And when I told my mother about it," Maria was continuing the story, "she was so mortified. Blamed herself for not teaching her daughter how to cook. She wanted to have a proper Italian dinner at her house to make up for it. But I had to leave or something, so it never happened." She bit into her shrimp and chewed thoughtfully. "You know, the way my game's been going, maybe it's time to trade my racquet in for a soup ladle."

"Are you serious?" Eve asked.

Maria didn't reply right away. Then she grinned. "No," she said with a return of cheerfulness.

Maria's friendly humor and openness were appealing. Eve found herself warming to the other woman.

Maria started describing an embarrassing moment in her last tournament in Sydney, Australia. At a crucial point, the sweatband around her forehead had slipped over her eyes.

"Like a blindfold," she said, illustrating by flashing her spread fingers across her eyes. "I see the ball bounce off Steffi's racquet and suddenly—nothing but blue terry cloth. So I push it up, go tearing crosscourt, and the damn thing's sliding all over my face. Finally I pull it down around my neck. People cheered."

"Did you make the point?" Eve asked.

"Yeah." Then ruefullly, "But I lost the match."

Sonorously, Loretta intoned. "It's not whether you win or lose, but how you play the game."

"Don't you believe it." Maria was now dead serious. "I used to be one of the top-seeded players. Now I'm fourteenth. In tennis, winning's what counts. Nothing else.

I've got to do well in Chicago to set me up for the U.S. Open." The Chicago tournament, Maria explained, was sponsored by Health Clubs International. "Not one of the biggies, but it's good prep for the Open so a lot of the top seeds will be there."

"So you'll be leaving again?" Eve asked.

Maria nodded. "Tomorrow, early. The way Glen's parties go, I probably should've brought my suitcase and gone right to the airport. But I'll break away early and get a few hours sleep."

Bo and Loretta went to refill their drinks, leaving the two younger women alone.

"Love your dress," Maria said. "So unusual. And those earrings are great."

Eve told her about Reva and the little shop in Greenwich Village.

"Maybe we can go together some time," Maria said.

"Sure." Eve would have preferred to dislike this woman, but it wasn't working out that way. *The story of my life lately*, Eve thought, *breaking out of clichéd patterns*.

"Where are you from?" Maria asked.

"Leonardtown. It's a small town in Maryland. Didn't Vic tell you?"

"No. He didn't tell me very much."

Eve wasn't surprised.

From his vantage point on deck, Vic looked at the two women, both attractive but so different. They seemed to be getting along. He wondered what they could be talking about. What did they have in common? Except him.

But that was a ridiculous thought. His long-term relationship with Maria couldn't be compared to this . . . this other infatuation. That's all it could be, he told himself, trying to minimize the attraction. Sure, Eve was a pretty woman, but he'd known others more beautiful. There was, however, that fascinating changeability, open and challenging one minute, seductively soft the next. Then to-night, something new again, exotic but disturbingly aloof. And so very, very tempting.

He'd been tempted before. In the past, he and Maria had often teased each other about such attractions. They had that kind of easy camaraderie. Apart for long periods, they'd allowed each other freedom. No recriminations. Nothing serious—until now. But a small town school-teacher was not the kind to dally with. Women like Eve Marsdon played for keeps.

It was after two in the morning and the party had thinned out considerably. Eve was in the lounge with a small group of the regular marina residents. Tired of standing, she'd followed Loretta's example and sat on the floor, her back to the couch, her legs tucked to the side. Loretta's voluminous muumuu provided easy modesty, but Eve's slit dress revealed an ample expanse of leg and thigh. Sitting on the couch in back of her, Glen kept glancing down, appreciating the view. Vic was standing at the bar. When some departing guests summoned Glen away, Vic immediately took his seat. Eve and Vic had not been alone at all, though Eve had often felt his gaze on her, even when she wasn't scanning the room to see where he was.

Eve became acutely aware of Vic's closeness, of his leg brushing against her arm. Once, when he leaned forward to respond to someone's question, he placed his hand briefly on her shoulder. A casual touch, but it sent a warm rush through her body.

"Hey, you guys," Maria called as she came over. "I've got to split. No, don't get up, Vic. Pauline and Sam are giving me a lift home."

Glen rushed up to her. "Darling," he pouted, "it's the shank of the evening. The party's just getting started."

"Take another look. Most people are gone. It's been

fun, but I've got a real early flight and I've got to get me some beauty sleep."

"You're beautiful enough," Glen said. "Besides, no one's fallen in the river yet," Glen said. "The party can't be over."

"Well, I can't wait," Maria said with a laugh. "Glen has this separation anxiety whenever a party breaks up," she told the others. She bent and gave Glen a peck on the cheek.

As she started to go, Eve felt Vic stir behind her. He stood. To stop Maria . . . to join her?

But Maria suddenly swerved. "Tell you what, if I win in Chicago, we'll have another party." Pleased with her idea, Maria spread her hands to the group. "Just this gang here, okay. I'll get my mother to cook us up one of her fabulous Italian feasts and we'll gorge ourselves on pasta and dance the tarantella."

"Marvelous," Glen said, amid echoing sounds of agreement.

"That way, I'll have all of you rooting for me," Maria announced. "Deal?"

"Sure . . . deal . . . you bet" came the replies.

Maria came over to give Loretta a good-bye hug. Eve started to get up. One of her legs had fallen asleep. Vic extended a hand to help and she rose awkwardly. "You'll come, won't you, Eve?" Maria said. "Take a break from cooking on that two-burner stove and help me celebrate my victory. Okay?"

Eve couldn't refuse such a friendly invitation. "Sure."

"Here's hoping there's a victory to celebrate," Glen said.

For a second, Maria's face fell. Then she shrugged. "Oh, what the hell? We'll have the party anyway."

Vic walked out with Maria.

A few minutes later Eve waved good-bye and slipped quickly away before Glen could give her an argument. She was almost to the end of Glen's pier when she saw the dark figure coming from the parking area. He waited for her.

"I'll walk you back," Vic said.

"You don't have to."

"I know."

"But you probably want to get back to the party."

"I don't." He took her arm and they started walking toward their pier.

"Did Maria get off okay?" A silly question, Eve realized as soon as she'd asked. And why did she even bring up Maria's name?

"Maria always gets off okay."

How did he mean that? Eve tried to read his expression, but his profile was unrevealing. He was keeping his hand locked under her elbow as they walked. She liked the feeling. They walked slowly. As they turned onto their pier, Eve's heel caught in a space between the planks and she stumbled. Vic caught her, thrusting her against him for a second. Eve's pulse halted, skipped, then raced tumultuously. He let her go and she averted her eyes.

"High heels," she explained in a too-bright voice meant to mask the effect he was having on her. She bent and removed her shoes.

"Shall I carry you," he asked.

"No."

"So you won't get a splinter," he said, reminding her of the intimacy of that little encounter.

Eve didn't need a reminder. "If I do, you'll just have to operate again."

"It'll be my pleasure."

By some tacit understanding that neither wanted this to end, their steps slowed even more. Somehow, after her stumble, he'd let go of her elbow and taken her hand, continuing to hold it as they walked. That, too, felt good. When they reached the *Six Pack* they stood facing each other. The electric light on the dock enclosed them in its circular glow. Eve felt fleetingly that she and Vic were completely alone in their world, with only darkness beyond. Eve looked up at Vic, at the shadowy planes of his face, his strong features, and the depths of those dark gray eyes. Then came a splash and a screeching laugh—intruding.

"That should be the grand finale of Glen's party," Vic said. "I think someone just fell into the river." There were sounds of yelling, then more laughter.

"Do you think they're all right?" Eve asked.

"Oh, sure. No one's ever drowned at one of Glen's bashes—except in liquor. Speaking of which, how about a nightcap?"

"I'm not sure I have anything to offer."

"Oh, you have a lot to offer," Vic said with soft insinuation. "But come on. I know where Al's tucked away some good brandy." He stepped onto the boat and held her hand while she followed. Eve found the key in her purse. He reached to take it, but Eve turned away, opened the door, lifted the hatch, and stepped down into the cabin. Vic followed.

"No more dropped keys," she said. "I don't make the same mistake twice."

"How reassuring."

He stood close to her. Eve saw him reach and held her breath, expecting his embrace. But what Vic was after was the bottle of Courvoisier he took out from the cabinet behind her.

"You bring the glasses," he said. On his way out, he picked up a couple of the outside foam cushions she stored inside at night.

Eve sighed, found a couple of glasses, and went above. Vic was sitting on the back bench, his long legs sprawled in front of him. "Sit right here," he said, patting the space next to him. "Everyplace else is damp."

Eve was glad to oblige. "No brandy snifters," she said. "These will have to do."

He took the two juice glasses and filled them half full.

Eve took hers. "What shall we drink to?"

"Happy days."

She'd have welcomed something more personal. She raised her glass, paused for a second to savor the heady aroma, then took a deep swallow.

"Easy," Vic cautioned. "That's potent stuff."

The warmth of the brandy ran through her. *Potent*, yes, but far more potent was the desire building in her. Darkness enhanced the intimacy, and the muffled sounds they heard seemed far away. They didn't talk at first. Eve sipped her drink, content to lean back and look at the stars, filling her senses with the surrounding night, the brandy, the closeness of the man beside her.

Vic started to tell her about the stars, pointing out the constellations. When he was a small boy, long before he'd studied astronomy and navigation, he'd learned such things from his father. "We'd go sailing at night sometimes," Vic said, "and he'd teach me how you could navigate by the stars."

Vic put down his drink to gesture and had his other arm on the cushion in back of Eve. His face was so close. She tilted her head back, touched his shoulder, and gradually let herself sink against him. Continuing to look as he talked, Eve heard, not words, but the timbre of his voice. After a while, he stopped talking. They sat quietly, but she could feel the tension building in him, feel it in the heightening response of her own body. The arm in back of her tightened and moved down to her waist.

If she twisted her head a little . . . like this . . . Vic's mouth was a whisper away. "Ohhh," she murmured softly to bridge the gap, and his mouth closed over hers. The kiss started gently as Vic inhaled the remainder of her sigh. Then slowly, his lips increased their pressure and demand, which Eve met with her own urgency. His tongue traced the outline of her mouth, darted between her lips and tangled with hers. His arms were around her now, his hands making roving patterns on her back, circling her waist, then moving higher to where his thumbs rubbed against the rise of her breasts.

She caught her breath when he suddenly released her mouth, but then sighed with pleasure to feel his lips trail over her cheeks, her closed lids, down to her throat and the wildly beating pulse in the hollow. His hand was caressing her breast in slow, circular motions. Ooooh . . . so . . . nice . . .

She heard him murmuring, "So sweet . . . Eve, you are so sweet," while his tongue tasted of that sweetness. Her senses were filled with him and clamoring for the ultimate fulfillment. For a second, a danger warning intruded into her consciousness. If she was beginning to love this man, she was in trouble. But the warning drowned in the maelstrom of surging desire.

She arched her body, leaning back and slightly turning her head from side to side. The silvery earrings tinkled. As if drawn to the sound, Vic kissed her ear. He nuzzled and licked until his tongue hit the silvery wires.

He drew back with a soft laugh. "I didn't count on a mouthful of metal."

Eve reached up to the offending ornaments. "I'll take them off."

His hands darted to cover hers. "Don't. I like them on you. You look different tonight, and very beautiful."

"How about exotic? I was trying for exotic."

"That, too." Vic stood and drew Eve up with him. He took her hands, raised them to his lips, and tenderly kissed each palm.

Eve wondered that such a gesture could be so sensual, warming her to her very toes.

Then, surprisingly, Vic dropped her hands and said, "I'd better go."

Eve stifled the protest that rose to her throat.

"Good night," Vic said, and bent to touch her mouth with a kiss. Eve fought the urge to reach up and hold him. He'd think her a clinging-vine type. Judging from Maria, that was not what he was used to. But hell—why should she ape the women Vic was used to? She would follow her own instincts.

Eve put her arms around Vic's neck and kissed him long and ardently. Then she stepped back, looked up at him, and smiled. "Good night," she said.

Vic gave her a quizzical look, hesitating. Eve understood his dilemma. But his self-control won out. He repeated his good night and departed. Eve didn't try to stop him. Whatever happened between them would have to come from both.

She watched his shadowed figure cross over to the *Hippolyta*. She was about to go below when she heard him call.

"Eve?"

"Yes."

"Would you like to learn how to sail?"

"Sure."

"First lesson tomorrow morning?"

"Sounds good to me." That was an understatement. Eve felt a rush of joy. That night, she slept soundly.

_____ SEVEN _____

By eight the next morning, they were on the river. Eve had intended for them to have breakfast on the _Six Pack_ before they left, but Vic was in a hurry. "Bring your Thermos of coffee and the muffins along and we'll have them later," he'd ordered. "Boat traffic's apt to get heavy by midmorning."

Eve doubted there'd be much boat traffic this morning. It was a cloudy day, with a breeze more like October than June. She'd been about to argue, but Vic had reminded her that _he_ was the captain, and she was only his mate. It crossed Eve's mind that her designation could have a double meaning, but she didn't mention this. She'd given him a snappy salute and a "Yessir", and followed orders.

They maneuvered out of the marina area under power. "Ready to start your lesson?" Vic asked.

Eve had been admiring his profile as he stood at the wheel, dark hair blowing, eyes scanning about. She was glad she'd brought a windbreaker to put on over her T-shirt and shorts, but Vic, in a white sport shirt and jeans, seemed not to feel the chill.

"Okay. Shoot," Eve told him.

Vic started talking about channels and depths and markers. He explained about the red and green buoys.

"Red right returning," Eve repeated. "That's easy to remember. So how come that one's on your left?"

"Because we're going out, not in," Vic patiently explained.

"Oh, right. Gotcha." Eve listened, trying to retain what he said. She didn't want him to think she was some lighthead. It *was* interesting, but there was so much. He had her look at a nautical chart and showed her where they were heading.

"The weather's iffy," Vic said, "so we won't go too far. With this wind, we'd better head south, downriver, see how far we get. Okay?"

"Fine with me." Of course, any direction would have been fine with Eve, as long as they were together.

A few minutes later, Vic called her to his side. "Take the wheel," he said.

"Who, me?"

"There's no one else on this boat, is there? I'm going to get the sails up."

"Oh, Vic, I don't think . . ."

"Just hold a steady course and head for that buoy up ahead."

She did. Uneasiness gave way to a good feeling. "Now cut the motor," Vic called when he had the mainsail up.

"How?"

"Turn the key. Like in a car."

She did. The motor sounds stopped and there was just the *whoof* of sail catching the wind. Beautiful. She kept the buoy dead ahead over the bow.

All of a sudden, Vic was pushing her aside. "I'd better take it," he said, and started turning the wheel to the left.

"Something wrong?"

He didn't answer right away, keeping his eyes ahead. When they were almost abreast with the buoy, now about fifteen feet to their starboard, Vic explained. "You were heading straight for that buoy."

"But you said to."

"I meant in that direction. Not to ram it."

Eve was indignant. "I wouldn't have."

"I'm sure you wouldn't. But under sail, the *Hippolyta* doesn't always respond with precision. It's okay. No harm done. Want to take the wheel again?"

"Yes. Yes, I do."

He seemed pleased. "Good."

She listened as he pointed out landmarks and showed where they were on the chart. "How about that breakfast now?" he said after a half hour and took the wheel while Eve went below to bring up two steaming mugs of coffee and a bag of blueberry muffins. She made the mistake of putting her half-eaten muffin down and having it snatched away by a marauding sea gull. She shook her fist at the thief, her anger an act to prompt Vic's laughter. She loved the sound of it. They both laughed a lot that morning. By midmorning they were in the busy area of the City Harbor and ahead of them was the Statue of Liberty.

The great lady was an awesome sight. Standing together at the wheel, neither Eve nor Vic spoke their admiration. They didn't have to. Vic's arm tightened around her. Eve looked up at him and smiled.

They continued into Upper New York Bay and its wider expanse of water. The wind was much lighter now. Vic continued Eve's lesson, describing how one had to respond to the changes in the prevailing wind. He explained about tacking, and how and when to come about and change direction.

"How can you tell when the wind changes?" Eve wanted to know.

"A natural sailor can feel it."

"I can't."

"That's why those telltales are up there on the mast." He pointed. "For unnatural sailors like you."

But his teasing was affectionate. Eve was eager to learn and put up with minor mishaps. Like back there when a big tugboat had gone by and Vic had shouted, "Wake coming." Instead of holding on, Eve had leaned way out to see and gotten tossed across the deck on her bottom. She now watched for the wake when a power boat crossed their path.

Around noon, the wind suddenly died. Reluctant to motor back, Vic maneuvered into a protected area away from commercial traffic and decided to drift for a while. He sent Eve below for more coffee. It gave her a chance to further explore the inside of the boat. While not as luxurious as Rader's yacht, the *Hippolyta* was quite commodious. The galley and lounge area were separate from the back cabin. A corner of the lounge was set up like a small office. Eve peeked into the other cabin. Nice—a real bed, built in drawers and closet and, best of all, the small bathroom, complete with a toilet, sink, and shower.

"Compared to the *Six Pack*, what you've got here is luxury," she told him.

"Everything's relative."

Eve started to tell him about her visit to the South Street Seaport and the photographs of how old-time sailors had to live. "Now *that* was roughing it," she concluded.

"You know, I've never been there."

"The Seaport? How come?"

"I've always thought of it as a tourist trap."

Eve scowled at him. "What if it is? It's also historical— and fun. You New Yorkers can get awfully jaded. This city has so much to offer. You need an out-of-towner to show you around."

Vic started to laugh. "Maybe you're right. Tell you what, I'll let you take me sometime. Deal?"

"Deal," she said, delighted by the prospect. Vic was drinking his coffee, and Eve suddenly realized he'd let go of the wheel. "Hey, who's driving the boat?"

"No one. This is what's known as the doldrums." He

narrowed his eyes, thinking back. "When I was a little kid, we had a small boat, a day sailor that my father'd built in the garage. We'd go sailing practically every day in the summer. Dad used to go nuts when we got caught like this. It sometimes took hours to get back, and my mother would be waiting and worrying."

"She didn't go with you?"

"No. She was afraid of boats, or the water, or both. Actually, I don't remember her very well. She died when I was eight. After that, it was just Dad and me."

"I'm sorry," Eve said. She remembered her own prosaic but happy childhood. "It must have been tough."

"It wasn't really. The two of us had a great time together. Everybody expected Dad would marry again, but he wasn't interested. Not that he lacked for female companionship," Vic said with a reminiscent chuckle. "I guess he didn't want to be tied down."

Like father, like son? Eve wondered.

As Vic went on talking, it was obvious to Eve how much he'd loved and admired his father. "He taught me everything I know about sailing. We had some great times together."

"Past tense?"

"He died ten years ago."

"I'm sorry." They were quiet for a while. Then Eve asked, "Do you take after him?"

"My father?" Vic thought about it. "In a way. I love to sail, if that's what you mean. But Dad had no head for business. He hated work and I don't. He had this little warehouse company and let other people run it. They did, right into the ground." Vic had taken over the almost-bankrupt business and turned it into a multimillion-dollar corporation. "It was fun," he told her. "I like things that offer a challenge."

"So do I," Eve said.

He seemed amused. "You?"

She bristled. "Yes, me!"

"What's the name of that little town you live in again?"

"Leonardtown. And if you're implying that small-town living lacks challenges, you are dead wrong. *Life* is a challenge, and you cosmopolites don't have a corner on drama and tragedy or love and excitement and success."

"I didn't mean . . ."

"Oh, yes, you did."

He gave her a long, searching look. "Maybe you're right. And if I've been patronizing you, I humbly apologize."

Eve's ire dissipated. He sounded sincere. "Okay, then. Apology accepted."

"Good." He took her by the shoulders and planted a kiss on her forehead. A comradely gesture, but the pressure of his fingers and the gleam in those gray eyes suggested an underlying passion kept in check—like hers was.

"I guess we'd better motor back," Vic said. "I give up on the wind."

Vic let her take the wheel at intervals. Under power, the trip was more straightforward, but noisier and lacking the grace of wind-filled white sails.

"It's more fun under sail," Eve told Vic when he came over to take the wheel.

He smiled, pleased, "Don't tell me I'm making a sailor out of you."

She gave him an answering grin. "Okay, I won't." He was doing a lot more than that. Being with Vic was changing her, releasing a pent-up longing for excitement, and for love, a longing she'd kept subdued for two years.

The aftermath of Graham's death had been a time for grieving. At first Eve had dwelled on the ordeal of his illness, her struggle to make his last days comfortable, to care for him at home while continuing with her work and attending to all the details that he'd always taken care of. Gradually, mercifully, those images had given way to happier memories of their early times together.

For a long time, Eve had lived with memories of past

happiness and past sorrow. But memories have a habit of losing their poignancy.

Oh, she had bounced back. Everyone remarked on how well the young widow was coping. She'd resumed her work and hobbies and social life, seeking the satisfactions they'd offered before. She would not let grief dominate her existence. But she was beginning to realize that "existing," not "living" was the proper word—as if she'd been marking time. Because Graham's death *did* mark a profound change in her life, but she hadn't wanted to acknowledge it, or perhaps, had seen no alternative to what she was doing. But there *were* alternatives. And her coming to New York this summer was her first step in seeking them out.

How Vic figured in all this she didn't know yet. But he'd already played a part. He'd challenged her personally and aroused her sexually, uncovering a reserve of passion she'd kept under wraps. And she was grateful. But what if she wanted more than he could give?

What Vic had told her today gave her an insight into the kind of man he was. His father as role model, the absence of a significant woman through most of his childhood—were these the reasons he was so damn independent, why he feared being tied to a woman? But there was Maria. Perhaps Maria held him by being careful not to try. Eve didn't think she could ever live that way. If she gave her love, it would have to be binding and forever. Could she pursue what was happening between her and Vic without getting hurt?

Vic had revealed a great deal in his conversation today, but there was still much they had to learn about each other. Eve suddenly realized that she'd never once mentioned Graham to him. Vic probably didn't even know she'd been married and was a widow.

"Hey, look," Vic said, pointing to the telltales and interrupting her reverie. "The wind's picked up."

This was not the time to tell him.

Vic put up the sails. The wind picked up even more, accompanied now by a pelting rain. Sailing upriver now, against the current, the *Hippolyta* churned up a heavy splashing spray. "Scared?" Vic asked.

"No." Vic's hair was whipping around and his face was dripping, but his eyes flashed and he wore the broad smile she loved. "What's to be scared of?" she cried.

His laugh blended with the sounds of wind and water. "Nothing," he replied.

Eve was sorry when they had to lower the sails and motor into the marina. After Vic backed into the slip, Eve followed orders and helped make the *Hippolyta* secure. By this time, the rain was coming down hard, and they scampered into the cabin. Eve was dry under her windbreaker, but Vic was soaked. He peeled off his shirt and tossed it aside. "How about some hot soup?" he asked, opening a cabinet. "Let's see. There's mushroom and tomato."

"Mushroom."

"I don't keep much food," Vic apologized. "I eat out mostly."

"Soup's fine."

It was. Vic found some wheat crackers, and they slurped their soup happily and noisily out of large mugs.

"Not exactly gourmet," Vic noted.

"Who cares?"

"You did well today."

"Did I?" She smiled her pleasure. "Thanks for taking me out." Eve had an idea. "Vic, how about I reciprocate tonight and take *you* out."

"Sailing?"

"Of course not. I'm not that good. Yet," she added with a grin. "Out to dinner. My treat."

"Sounds good to me."

She was elated by his prompt acceptance. "But I get to choose the place."

"Okay. Where?"

"The Rainbow Room. And don't tell me it's a tourist place, because I don't care. I've always wanted to go. It's got tradition and it'll be fun."

"If that's your choice."

"It is." Eve finished her soup in one last, satisfying gulp. "Thanks. I needed that. And what I need next is a nice hot shower." She peered out the window at the driving rain. "All the way up there," she added, picturing the long walk up to the bathhouse.

"You can shower here," Vic offered.

"I wasn't hinting . . ."

"Don't be silly. Why wade through all that? In fact, use the shower whenever you want while you're here. The galley, too."

The offer surprised her. "I couldn't impose."

"No problem. I'm working most days. You'd have the place to yourself."

His presence would be a more attractive inducement, Eve thought. "I accept," she said. "At least for this once."

"Good."

The hot shower felt wonderful. She rubbed herself dry with the oversize bath towel, heightening the sensitivity of her skin. Wrapping herself in the towel, she emerged and looked with distaste at the damp clothes she'd stripped off and dropped on the bed. But lying next to her things was a man's velour robe. Vic must have put it there. Eve put it on, gratefully, caught sight of herself in a mirror on the door, and started to laugh.

It was ridiculously big, trailing at least a foot on the floor. Her head emerged turtlelike from the rolled collar. The belt, because of the loops through which it was threaded, rode low on her hips and created a V neck that reached down to her navel. Taking the belt out and tying it around her waist helped some, but not much. Still, it was soft and comfortable with a faintly masculine smell.

She ventured outside. Vic was just putting down the phone.

"I made a reservation for—" He interrupted himself to smile at the picture she presented.

"I assume you meant this for me," she said.

He nodded.

"It's not quite my size, but thanks."

"You look charming, and very sexy." His voice was an octave lower.

She gestured expansively with hands hidden by voluminous sleeves. "Like this? Covered from nose to toes?" With a breathy laugh, she said, "Look at me. I'm talking in rhymes."

He'd come closer. "I am looking." With both hands, he smoothed her wet hair away from her face. "I like what I see."

His eyes seemed to have changed color, the gray softened by an underlying silvery glow. Vic's fingers brushed a tender path down her cheeks and rested on her shoulders. His arms were muscular and strong, and the skin on his bare chest gave off a golden gleam. His eyes drew hers again, and Eve felt caught by the desire she saw there.

Eve knew she could avert her gaze, pull back, and break the spell. Perhaps this was wrong for her, perhaps she was letting herself in for future hurt . . .

But the present moment was all that mattered. Eve didn't want to play it safe. She wanted Vic. He saw the corroboration he sought in her eyes. At the touch of his lips, a hot, surging need engulfed her. No gentle build-up this time. Their kiss was searing in its passion. Their lips clung, clashing tongues exchanging fiery messages of desire. He dropped his head to find the pulse in her throat; his tongue accelerated its wild beating. Eve pressed her palms to his bare shoulders. She felt a churning warmth building inside her, then a weakness in her legs that drove her against the hard plains of his body.

The hem of her robe got pinned underfoot, the belt

giving way and loosening her robe. Vic spread it wider apart, his hands gliding over her bare skin, sending shivers of pleasure through her. When he reached and cupped her breasts, she sighed, then gasped as his mouth came down to cover one rosy peak. Eve stroked his tangled hair and pressed him closer. Vic raised up and slipped the robe from her shoulders. It fell in a soft heap around her feet. As he gazed at her nakedness, she saw the erection thrusting against his tight jeans. Vic held her a few inches away, his look fiercely questioning.

Eve understood. "Yes," she said softly. As if there could be any other response.

There was elation in his smile. He quickly undid his belt and in seconds had shed his jeans. Eve caught her breath at the sinewy strength of his body and the jutting evidence of his arousal. He drew her close, molding her yielding softness to him. Eve clasped her hands behind his neck as they kissed. His mouth still on hers, Vic raised her off her feet and went into the inner cabin. Eve put her legs up to straddle him. Vic kicked the door closed behind them and Eve caught their reflection in the mirror.

How wanton! Like women in the movies. Eve, for whom married sex had been satisfying but sedate, had never felt like this before. Vic laid her on the bed and turned to close the blinds. When he went to light the bedside lamp, she raised a restraining hand.

"Don't."

"But I want to see you when we make love," he said softly. "I want the whole experience."

Eve realized that she did, too. Why deny herself the visual pleasure of his masculinity? Lamplight turned his skin amber and made sensuous the curves of his chest and hips and buttocks.

Vic lay down beside her. He didn't speak, but let his fingers and lips and tongue express his need and his passion. And how eloquently he delivered his message. He covered her with kisses, his tongue darting and exploring the curves and niches of her body while his hands roved with tantalizing expertise to mold and caress and tease. He filled her senses; she saw and tasted and breathed and felt him. The sum of all this was the creation of a far more overpowering sensation. What Eve felt was love. She was in love with Vic Adesso.

Eve sought to express her feeling, to use her body, now so sensitive and responsive, to make love to Vic. She became daring, following his example, giving herself the freedom to touch and caress and kiss. She breathed her heat into his ears and tested the depth of his navel with her hot tongue. Her fingers curled into the cluster of hair on his chest and trailed down the V pattern to the bushiness around his penis. Inflaming him, Eve was fueling her own frenzied desire.

"My darling," she said, and the endearment ended Vic's restraint. He pushed her back on the bed and raised himself over her, holding himself away for a second as he looked into her eyes. He kissed her deeply and Eve felt his pressure between her thighs. She spread her legs, and he entered her. Against his lips, she uttered a small cry of pain. It had been so long. Vic held still, then eased into her gently. Very soon, the pain disappeared and the spiral of pleasure was starting.

Vic took his time. As her urgency mounted, Eve started to move against him, encouraging him to penetrate more deeply. She clasped her legs around him, picking up his rhythm. He pushed further into her and Eve twisted and arched, her outer movements reflecting the coiling undulations deep inside her. "No . . . yes . . . more . . . oh . . . please . . . more . . . oh, please, please . . ."

Her fingers dug into him. Eve's last cry strangled as she felt an agonizing tightening and then a shattering release. She closed her eyes, flinging her head from side to side, clinging to Vic and crying his name. When she opened her eyes, he was staring with wonderment. Then he renewed his rhythmic thrusting with a fierceness that brought him quick, triumphant release.

They stayed locked together as the tension ebbed from their bodies, sated and bathed in a mist of happiness.

They slept for a while. Vic felt a tingling and awakened. He had his arm around Eve; her head nestled into the crook of his shoulder. His fingers were falling asleep, but he didn't want to disturb her. She looked so sweetly innocent, her black hair tousled and still wet, like a child.

But she wasn't a child. Their lovemaking had proven that. She was all woman. But a woman who defied any set definition. Wholesome or exotic, naive or sophisticated, agreeable or willful. But there was no *either/or*. Eve was all of the above.

When she'd come out swathed in that oversize man's robe, all shining and squeaky clean, she'd been like a seductive cherub, tempting and sweet. But the cherub had metamorphosed into a temptress who fired his blood. And the temptress had become the lovely woman whose gratified pleasure became part of his own fulfillment. In Vic's experience, sex was a pleasurable but usually selfish activity, with each participant striving for individual fulfillment. Even furthering the other's pleasure was usually motivated by ego, not love. Vic had given more of himself in this act of love with Eve than ever before.

Act of love? Vic frowned. Why attach any special significance to what had happened? Good sex was good sex, without the need of romantic overtones. He tried to ease his arm from under her.

Eve awoke, looked up at him, and smiled. Immediately he felt the stirrings of desire. "Sorry to wake you. My arm was falling asleep."

"Red right returning," she said sleepily.

"What?"

"I was dreaming. We were sailing, and I had to guide

us home but there were too many colored buoys and I couldn't remember 'red-right-returning.'"

"What happened?"

"I don't know. You woke me up."

"Sorry." He bent and kissed the tip of her nose. "If you have the dream again, you'll know."

"What time is it?"

"Almost six. Our reservation at the Rainbow Room's for seven."

"Mmm," she murmured, nuzzling against his chest. Then she gave him a mischievous smile. "We could cancel . . ."

"Not on your life." Vic sat up and withdrew from temptation. She looked so very appealing, and the memory of her lovemaking . . .

But he didn't like having his mind befogged by passion. The intensity of his attraction disturbed him. "You're not welshing on your offer. You promised me a fancy dinner and I aim to collect."

If she was disappointed, she didn't show it. "Right you are," she said. She got out of bed. Vic almost lost his resolve as he watched her put on her clothes.

"You're peeking," she accused.

"Ogling's more like it," he admitted. "You have a lovely body."

She flushed, and finished dressing. Pausing at the door, she asked, "How much time do I have?"

"Just yell when you're ready."

"Will do," she said, and disappeared.

Vic looked at the warm space she'd vacated. Was he being a damn fool—or what?

EIGHT

Vic usually avoided places like the Rainbow Room. He thought of them as tourist meccas and settings for engagement parties and postprom dates.

"So what's wrong with that?" Eve argued as they were whizzed up in one of Rockefeller Center's elevators. "They're happy occasions. Special . . . like this."

"How come special?"

She enumerated. "First time in the Rainbow Room, first lesson sailing, and . . ." Eve hesitated, not sure how to define her first time with Vic, or *if* she should define it at all. But the elevator stopped and she didn't have to.

They were being shown to their table when a busboy darted by, saw Eve, and did a double take. He grinned and waved. It was a transformed Jason, the young man she had met at the New School, minus his earring and neon colored clothes.

"Who's your friend?" Vic asked.

Eve explained how she'd met Jason. "Come to think of it, he mentioned his father was a chef at the Rainbow Room."

"Is that why you chose this place?"

"No. I've always wanted to come here, but somehow it never happened—until tonight."

When they were seated, Eve scanned the room, her eyes sparkling with delight. The elegance and beauty of the restaurant was just as she'd imagined. Through the surrounding windows, their table for two afforded a panorama of Manhattan, a magical, glittering wonderland.

"What a glorious view," Eve said when the maître d' left them. "He gave us the best table."

"A tribute to how lovely you look."

"Or the bill I saw you slip him."

"I prefer my version," Vic said with a smile.

"So do I." Luckily, she'd thought to pack this linen summer suit. It was just dressy enough, with its shaped emerald-green jacket and high-waisted black split skirt.

"That green matches your eyes, and your earrings. Emeralds, are they?"

Graham's last present to her. Eve hesitated, reluctant to seize the opening, afraid of spoiling the harmony of this night. But she wanted to tell Vic about herself, to deepen their intimacy beyond the purely physical.

"Yes. They were a present from Graham, my husband."

His dark brows rose with surprise. "You're married?"

"I *was* married. Graham died two years ago."

"I'm sorry."

"That I'm a widow?"

"Yes . . . no." He was frowning. "I mean I certainly wouldn't want to have spent the afternoon in bed with a woman whose husband was alive. That sounds terrible. But you know what I mean."

"It's all right. I understand."

He shook his head. "You're confusing me. Why didn't you tell me before?"

"No special reason. I mean, I couldn't just come up with a 'By the way, I'm a widow,' could I?"

"Why not?"

"The subject didn't come up. I'm sure you never felt the need to disclose all your love affairs."

"Touché. I get the point. But I was never married. There's a difference."

"So there is."

"Hey, Eve, how goes it?" It was Jason carrying a pitcher of water.

"Fine, Jason. How are you?"

"Well, there's lotsa places I'd rather be than here in this nerdy jacket," Jason said. He glanced over his shoulder. "I better look busy." He reached for Eve's glass which was still full, emptied the contents into his pitcher, then proceeded to fill it again, very slowly. "My father's brainstorm," he told them. "Dad's got this thing about work ethics."

"I think your father probably said *work ethic*," Vic smilingly corrected.

"Jason, this is a friend of mine, Victor Adesso."

"Hiya. Yeah, work ethic . . ." Jason proceeded to administer to Vic's glass in the same way, all the while talking in a furtive sotto voice. "Plus, I think he kinda likes us working together. Not that we're really together, but you know . . ." Eve nodded. "It's only two nights a week and the pay's good, so what the hell?" Eve's eyes flashed a warning that the waiter was coming. "Yeah, right." Jason had a last bit of advice. "Hey, order the rack of lamb. It's Dad's specialty. He does it great." Jason went on to the next table.

The waiter gave them a few more minutes to study the menu, then returned to take their order. They had both decided on the terrine appetizer and a house salad. "And for the entrée, sir?" the waiter asked.

Vic's look asked and received Eve's confirmation.

"The lady and I will have the rack of lamb." With a flourish, Vic closed the menu and added. "We have it on good authority that the chef does it great."

"Of course, sir."

Vic and Eve grinned at each other. The short encounter with Jason seemed to have relaxed Vic again. By the time they had their first glass of champagne, he was at ease and they talked comfortably together. Her disclosure had apparently opened the door to his curiosity. He plied her with questions about her childhood, her life with Graham, his illness and how she had coped with it.

Eve didn't resent the questions. She was glad of Vic's interest, and wanted him to know. Even describing Graham's losing battle with leukemia wasn't painful. The heartache was past and her memories no longer focused on sadness and loss. Vic's gaze turned speculative at times, as though he tried to picture her in the circumstances she was describing.

And she got Vic to talk more about himself, his ambition in high school to study marine engineering and how he'd changed to a finance major in college in order to go in with his father. School vacations, she gathered, had usually been travel jaunts, often with one of his father's lady friends along. Not like the family reunions Eve remembered.

"They were fun when I was a kid, and later as an adult," Eve told him. "But in between, through high school and part of college—deadly. I'd have gladly traded places with you. Dave and I, he's my cousin, used to commiserate with each other." Their discovery that her cousin was the Dave Bittner who had played college football with Vic at Northwestern set them to laughing.

"If I remember right," Vic said, "Dave once invited me home with him for spring break." He laughed as he reached across the table to take Eve's hand. "You and I might have met . . . let's see . . . about sixteen years ago."

She scowled. "I was twelve, with braces. You didn't miss a thing."

His fingers were caressing. Eve absorbed the warmth of his smile. "I don't know about that," he said.

Their dinner was superb. "You've got a healthy appetite," Vic observed.

"It's been a strenuous day." Realizing how he could take that, Eve flushed.

His teasing, "Did I tire you out?" didn't help.

"I was hungry, not tired," she said tartly. "After a whole day on a blueberry muffin . . . correction, *half* a muffin—that thieving gull got the other half—and a cup of soup, what do you expect?"

He grinned. "With you, I'm never sure what to expect."

"That's part of my charm." She didn't wait for him to agree, or disagree.

Jason was back with his water pitcher. He looked at their empty plates and gave a satisfied grin. "See, I didn't steer you wrong."

"You certainly didn't," Eve told him. "The lamb was fabulous."

"Our compliments to the chef," Vic added.

"Yeah, I'll tell him. Dad says the kitchen's one of the best in the city. This here's a pretty nice place, except for the Stone Age music." He made a face. "Like to vomit." A waiter at another table was beckoning to him. "I gotta go. Catch ya later."

The orchestra had launched into a medley of old Sinatra songs, the cozy dancing kind. "Don't tell Jason," Eve said, "but I go for Stone Age music. Would you like to dance?"

"Sure, but I warn you . . . I'm better on a boat deck than a dance floor."

"It doesn't matter."

What mattered was being in his arms, moving in unison to the romantic strains of the music. Actually, they danced well together. Following Vic seemed effortless as her body easily anticipated his lead. She nestled against him and closed her eyes. Dancing was such a sensual experience.

For Vic, too, she realized as his arm tightened around her and she sensed his arousal.

The medley ended. They returned to their table and the waiter brought dessert, an elegant chocolate mousse cake. "We didn't order this," Vic said.

"Compliments of Chef Pomeranz." With an exaggerated shrug, he added, "And Busboy Pomeranz."

Jason waved at them from his station.

It was a delectably sweet confection. Eve lingered over coffee, wanting to prolong the evening. They talked quietly until Eve was distracted by a flurry around them. Nearby, a foursome of new arrivals was attracting attention as the maître d' seated them. "That tall redhead, he looks familiar," Eve said.

Vic turned. "Boris Becker. And the one who needs a shave, that's Andre Agassi."

The two glamorous young women with the tennis stars were all smiles when a photographer started snapping pictures.

"That's another thing I don't like about these places," Vic said with a frown. "All the picture-taking."

"I think it's fun," Eve said.

But a few minutes later she changed her mind. They were enjoying their mousse when suddenly a flashbulb exploded right at them. Then a voice called, "How about a smile, Vic? And the lady?" The flash caught them again.

"Cut that out," Vic ordered. The photographer came to the table, hovered over them, and started asking questions.

"Adesso, isn't it? Victor Adesso? We met last year at the Virginia Slims matches. Remember?"

"No."

"Sure. You were with Maria Spezia that time. And a lot of other times. Right?"

"I don't know who you are . . ."

"Hal Janowitz, photojournalist. I follow the sports scene."

"This is *not* part of the sports scene, Mr. Janowitz."

"What I meant was, I follow sports people. You know, little human interest items about their lives . . . and their romances. Get me?"

Eve could see Vic's anger mounting.

"What I'd like right now is to get you away from me. Good-bye, Mr. Janowitz."

"C'mon, gimme a break. Is it all over between you and Maria? Or just another temporary cooling off like last year?"

"I told you . . ."

"But you're not telling me anything," the man wheedled. "Come on. Is this a new romance?" He rested one hand on the table and bent over Eve. "What's your name, little lady?"

"None of your business," she shot back.

Janowitz turned to Vic. "Spunky, isn't she?"

"Get out of my face, Janowitz," Vic said, his voice low and coldly threatening.

The photographer backed away. "Jesus, what's the big deal? Afraid Maria'll find out? If you wanted hush-hush, you shouldn't've picked the Rain—" He stopped as Vic half rose from his chair. "Okay, I'm going. What's the big deal?" He left.

"Sorry about that," Vic told Eve.

"You couldn't help it."

"Maria says you get used to that kind of thing." He shook his head. "I can't."

"It goes with the territory, I guess. Maria's a public figure."

"With a right to some privacy, like the rest of us. At least he didn't get your name."

Who was Vic trying to protect, her or Maria?

The maître d' came over. "Is everything all right, sir?" he asked Vic.

"Fine."

But Eve knew it wasn't. The joy had gone out of the evening.

On the way out, they passed Jason. Eve thanked him for sending over the dessert. "Dad's idea, but I picked which one," Jason said. "Next time you come, it'll be this ice-cream cake thing that gets set on fire, okay?"

"Sure." But Eve wondered if there would be any next time.

On the drive back to the Marina, Vic's conversation was impersonal, with comments on the weather report, the crime problems in Central Park at night, the mayoral election coming up in the city.

His good-night kiss outside the *Six Pack* was tender, but brief. He started to go, but her hand on his arm detained him. "Vic . . ." Eve hated the tremor in her voice. "Vic . . ." she began again. "There's something I need to know. Are you and Maria Spezia lovers?"

It seemed an eternity until his answer. "We have been," he said.

"I see." There was nothing more to say. "Good night."

Eve had anticipated an entirely different ending to this day. Instead of falling asleep in Vic's arms, she tossed for hours on her narrow bed.

She had to back off. That was all there was to it. She couldn't let herself love a man who was involved with another woman.

When Eve came out on deck the next morning, Vic was talking to Bo at the end of their dock. He saw her and waved, but headed right for his car and drove off. Apparently he was ready to forget what had happened between them yesterday. She wished *she* could.

Late that afternoon, he returned. Eve didn't see him at first. She was working on her stone on shore, totally engrossed in what her chisel was uncovering. The contours were beginning to suggest a form. Soon she would know what this stone was meant to be.

Too bad, she thought, you couldn't get to the heart of people this way—just chip away at the exterior and discover the truth underneath.

Vic's voice startled her. He was standing just behind her. "Interesting shape," he commented.

"I'm not into shaping it yet, just cleaning it up to see what's there."

"Could be a lot of things." He walked around the table, looking through narrowed eyes. "Depends on where you look from."

"And who's doing the looking."

"Eye of the beholder?" He turned his gaze to her. "Yeah, I guess so." He touched her cheek. "You're smudged."

"I know." She wanted to push his hand away . . . wanted to grab it and hold his palm against her face, her lips. Contradictions. Eve didn't know what she wanted to do.

Loretta was coming toward them. Vic dropped his hand. "That's a heavy stone. Did you carry it up?"

"Bo brought it."

"Bo's gone by now. Want me to take it back for you?"

She searched his face for something other than politeness, but saw only cloudy gray eyes and a slight frown. "Maybe later," she said.

"I'll be leaving again in a half hour . . . business dinner."

Eve felt an inner tightness. So the man had a busy life. She forced a bright smile and said curtly, "Don't worry. I'll manage."

Vic matched her tone. "Okay then."

"Hi," Loretta greeted them. "I just caught the sports news. Maria made the semifinals. I think we're gonna have us a celebration."

"I heard," said Vic. He gave a slight wave and walked off.

"Did I interrupt something?" Loretta asked.

"Not really."

"Problems?"

"No." Eve turned back to her stone.

Loretta was studying her. "You like him, don't you?"

"Vic?" Eve picked up a rasp. "Sure I like him. He's been a real help." She filed away furiously.

"You know that's not what I'm talking about." Quiet. Eve wasn't answering. "And you'd better watch how you're digging away at that one spot," Loretta cautioned.

"Oh, damn." Eve threw down the rasp. Another minute and she'd have made an ugly gouge.

"I mean, you *really* like him," Loretta said.

"So?" But Loretta's look of affection and sympathy diffused Eve's belligerence.

"So nothing," said Loretta cheerfully. "I think it's great. Go for it, kid."

"It's not that easy."

"It never is, but go for it anyway."

Greta gave her the opposite advice that night. "Eve, I think you ought to just pack up and go home," she said after inspecting the *Six Pack*. They'd had a date to go out to dinner together, and Greta and George had come by for a drink first. "This is hardly bigger than a rowboat."

"You're exaggerating again. In fact, I'm quite comfortable."

"And where's that Adesso guy live?"

Eve pointed. "Right there."

"Practically on top of you."

If you only knew, she thought silently, then scowled at her own sick joke.

Greta's attention was drawn to someone coming down the dock. "Look," she whispered. "I think that's the other one. He *does* look like Fred Astaire."

It was Glen Rader. Eve introduced them, and Glen immediately proceeded to turn on the charm. He managed to invite himself out to dinner with them at Mercutio's and picked up the check, which impressed George. "We must do this again soon," he said as they were saying good-bye outside the restaurant, and then had another idea. Eve and the Avedons must come for a short jaunt on his boat that weekend, then dinner afterward, he said. He wouldn't take no for an answer. They agreed.

"Not a bad dude," George remarked as he and Greta were driving Eve back.

Greta was skeptical. "A little too smooth and dandified for my taste."

"Which is why you married me, sweetheart," George told her.

"The other extreme," Greta muttered. To Eve, she said, "But he certainly seems to go for you."

"Glen Rader," Eve said, "goes for whoever's available."

"A New York playboy," Greta decided. "Be careful."

Eve shrugged off the warning. "I can handle Glen."

"And the other one?"

Vic was a different story, not the kind of man who could be *handled*. Before Eve could think of an answer, her friend said, "Eve, don't get involved."

She should have heeded Greta's earlier warnings. But at least she could limit her losses, Eve thought. She had no intention of abandoning her plans and running back to Leonardtown. So she and Vic had enjoyed an interlude of making love. Two mature people setting off some sexual fireworks. Certainly not a rare occurrence. Or was it?

Eve had to acknowledge that, for her, it had been rare and wonderful, quelling any vague notions she'd had of a fling to add zest to her summer. She would just have to hold the relationship in check. Cynically, Eve guessed that Vic would cooperate.

"Good morning." Vic called. He was stepping off his boat just as Eve came out. "I was about to knock on your door."

He walked over. Eve had hardly seen Vic in the past

two days, so this early-morning visit surprised her. Well, hardly a visit. He was keeping his distance, talking to her from the dock with one foot on the *Six Pack*. It was hot again so he'd left off the tie, but he was dressed for work in a lightweight summer suit. He looked marvelous. And here she was in old wrinkled shorts and shirt.

"I'll be staying in the apartment for a couple of days," Vic said. "Business."

She believed him; Maria was still in Chicago.

"All right." Why was he telling her? He certainly didn't need Eve's permission. "Is there something you want me to do?"

The question put a wry smile on his face, but it was fleeting.

"No. I thought I'd leave you the key to the *Hippolyta*. Remember we talked about your using the shower and galley if you wanted."

She remembered all too well the occasion of his offer. "Thanks, but . . ."

He didn't let her finish. "Make life a little easier for yourself. Here, catch." He threw before she could protest.

Eve missed and the key landed in front of her.

"We'll have to work on those catching skills," he said.

Eve picked up the key, considered tossing it back, then decided not to. No reason why she shouldn't take him up on his offer, since he wouldn't be around. "Thanks."

"Eve . . . ?"

Her heart gave a tumble. There was something in his voice . . .

But after a long pause all he said was, "Call on Bo if you need anything."

"Sure." As he turned to go, something masochistic made her ask, "Have you heard from Maria?"

"Yeah. She's playing Garrison today. Final match."

"So she'll be back soon."

"Probably. With Maria, you never know."

Was that part of Maria's attraction, Eve wondered, that

she was unpredictable? Probably the last thing he wanted was a woman who prized constancy and commitment.

Eve watched Vic's loping stride down the dock. Damn the man for looking so attractive. And why hadn't she put on something other than this grimy outfit this morning?

Because, she reminded herself, she was running out of fresh clothes. "Get thee to the laundry room," she muttered, and went into the cabin to gather up what needed washing.

The chore took all morning. There was only one washer and dryer and Gina, the young pregnant woman from the *Four Leaf Clover*, had gotten there first. They started talking, and Eve asked Gina about her solo trip across the Atlantic in a twenty-six-foot sailboat.

"There were some pretty hairy episodes," Gina said and proceeded to describe them.

"Weren't you scared?" Eve asked.

"Sure."

"So why'd you do it?"

"It was something I'd always dreamed of doing. You don't *not* do something just because there's going to be some scary times, not if it's really important to you." Gina patted her belly. "Hey, having a kid is pretty scary. I don't mean only the delivery, the whole business of being a parent. But you do it, don't you?"

"I don't have children." *Yet*, Eve added to herself.

"That was a rhetorical question," Gina said. "But I'll bet there's something you really want to do, isn't there?"

Eve used the excuse of the dryer's clicking off to deflect the question. "Right now, I'll settle for some clean clothes."

After Gina had gone and while waiting for her own laundry to dry, Eve sat, thumbing through a copy of yesterday's paper that someone had left. But her thoughts kept returning to what Gina had said. A remarkable young woman, one who went after what she wanted and met the challenges straight on.

Of course, their situations were totally different. But maybe the particular situation wasn't important. It was an attitude, a way of confronting life. Eve had faced challenges in the past, and some, like Graham's illness, that couldn't be conquered. But she'd persevered.

Eve closed the newspaper and was about to put it down when a picture on the back sports page caught her eye. Maria Spezia in a triumphant pose, holding her racquet high above her head. Every inch the champion. The caption read, "Spezia victorious again. Takes on Garrison tomorrow."

There were all kinds of challenges, Eve thought.

The laundry room wasn't air-conditioned. By the time Eve got back to the *Six Pack* with her pile of laundry, she was soaked through. She'd fold everything later. First some iced tea, even if she had to chip chunks from her block of ice. But on the *Hippolyta* were real ice cubes, and the shower she needed. Why not? She took the key Vic had given her and went over.

His telephone rang just as Eve was opening the door. Should she answer? But she couldn't ignore the persistent summons. It might be Vic.

Maria's voice startled her. "Vic's not here," Eve told her, and launched into an explanation of why she was on Vic's boat. Maria, happily uninterested, interrupted. "Eve, I won," she cried. "Back to my old form. I beat Garrison. Isn't that great?"

"Great."

"So look, the victory dinner's on. I called Mom and it's all set. She's thrilled. Probably started her cooking the minute I hung up. That's the good part. Seven o'clock tomorrow at her house. The bad part is that it's in Brooklyn." Maria waited for Eve to make a note of the Ocean Parkway address. "If you'll tell Loretta, she'll get the word out to the others, okay?"

"Sure."

"And don't forget Glen. He'd be furious if he was left

out. Though maybe when he hears Brooklyn, he'll change his mind." Maria's laugh was boisterous.

"I don't have his number."

"Bo does. Oh, I just missed Vic at his office. I thought he might've ducked out and gone back there, but I guess not."

"He's not here."

"I'll have to call back later then."

"Vic said something about staying over in the apartment for a couple of days."

"Okay. I'll phone him there. I want to tell him myself."

"Of course."

Eve hung up. She sat for a moment, looking at the telephone, picturing the woman who'd just been at the other end—laughing, elated by the victory she'd just come from, still in her stylish tennis whites. *She probably doesn't even look sweaty*, Eve thought, pulling at the shirt that was sticking to her skin.

Naturally Maria would want to share her happy news with her lover.

Eve gave out a puffy sign. She would have her shower, then go find Loretta and Bo to give them Maria's message about the party. She wished she didn't have to go. A wish, she realized, that was easily fulfilled. She could make up an excuse and spare herself the ordeal.

But that could be the wrong approach. Maybe seeing Maria and Vic together right now was the painful antidote she needed. Never before, Eve thought ruefully, had she thought of love as requiring an antidote.

NINE

Geraldine Spezia, Maria's mother, was an earthy, blunt woman who served a liberal assortment of pithy sayings along with her fabulous Italian food.

"Northern Italian," she explained, when someone commented on her and her daughter's blondness. "Everyone thinks all Italians are dark like Victor. The farther south, the darker they get."

"Not that my mother's prejudiced," Maria said with a laugh.

"I'm not. I just tell the truth," Mrs. Spezia declared. "Northern Italians are better looking and better cooks. That's all." Brooking no argument, she went back to her kitchen to fetch still another platter for the lavish buffet.

Her house was old style, with big, comfortable rooms. The front porch led into the living room which adjoined a large dining room where the table had been placed against the back wall so people could help themselves.

Eve came with Glen Rader, who had insisted on picking her up. He'd gotten lost and they'd arrived late, with Glen making a dramatic entrance, exclaiming, "It's like driving in a foreign country. Even the language is different— Brooklynese."

Vic had looked surprised to see her with Glen. Maria, glowing in an orange dress that dramatized her tan, was an effervescent hostess, flitting happily among her guests.

Eve was glad it was a large gathering so she could just stand back and observe. Apparently the party had grown from Maria's original intent. There were a dozen people from the marina, some Spezia neighbors and relatives, and a tennis contingent that included a couple of personalities whom Eve recognized. There was also Dave Fenster, Maria's coach, who'd come with his wife, and Tanya Czernak, Maria's doubles partner, plus a stocky, sandy-haired man, Frazier Doyle, the owner of a New Hampshire ski resort.

At first Eve thought Frazier was Tanya's date, but he seemed more interested in Maria. It was Frazier who was constantly at Maria's side, helping her serve and pass drinks, with Mrs. Spezia beaming approval from the sidelines. What was going on here? If Vic noticed, he didn't seem to object.

Vic came over. "I thought you'd be coming with Loretta and Bo."

"Glen was kind enough to offer me a ride."

"Good old Glen." There was no missing the sarcasm. Vic nodded in Glen's direction. "Always looking out for the ladies." Glen was engaged in animated conversation with Tanya. "Or is it *on the lookout*?"

"You don't like him."

"I don't trust him."

And neither should you, his tone implied.

"Let's just say," Vic added, "that Glen's track record with women hasn't been exactly exemplary."

"He's been very nice to me," Eve said with a shrug. She was capable of making her own judgments. She changed the subject. "Thanks for giving me free run of the *Hippolyta*."

"You've used it? Good."

"Remind me to return your key."

"Why? Keep it," he said.

"You're staying on in the apartment?" *With Maria?* was the unspoken part of her question.

"No."

Sending his eyes boring into her, Eve looked up and was drawn into their smoky depths. For a second, the voices and clatter around them faded and they were alone. But only for a second.

"Vittorio." It was Mrs. Spezia. "Come help me with the drinks. I offer Strega and Lambrusco, and these people ask for Bloody Marys and Rusty Nails. "Such names . . .""

"Can I get you a drink?" Vic asked Eve.

"Later. I'm going to get some of that delicious food first."

Mrs. Spezia approved. "A wise young woman. And pretty, too," she added, giving Eve a thorough inspection and jabbing Vic for confirmation. "Right, Vittorio?"

"Undeniably."

"Don't use big words. Just say yes."

Their ease with each other indicated long familiarity. But Eve wondered if the older woman really approved. Mothers usually wanted their daughters safely married. Had Mrs. Spezia bought into the new morality?

"Maria, she tells me you live by Vittorio on a boat," Mrs. Spezia said. "Crazy."

"I kind of like it."

"Bobbing up and down on the water? What is there to like?"

Eve laughed. "It's really not bad, and there are compensations."

Mrs. Spezia's shrewd appraisal went from Eve to Vic and back again. "Uh huh. I see."

Eve felt uncomfortable and was relieved when Maria joined them. She didn't want Mrs. Spezia to elucidate on what it was she saw.

When her mother left with Vic in tow, Maria asked Eve, "Has Mama pried any secrets out of you yet?"

Startled by the question, Eve said no, that they'd hardly talked.

"She's slipping," Maria said with a laugh. "My mother has this terrible habit of asking the most personal questions the minute she meets a person. Don't let her bother you."

"No problem," Eve said. "I like her. She's a real down-to-earth lady."

"Who's sure she knows exactly what's best for everyone, especially her wayward daughter. Not that I listen. I've been ignoring her advice for years."

Eve detected a rueful note in Maria's voice. "She wants you to be happy."

With a pensive frown, Maria said, "I thought I was." The frown changed to a bright smile. "Come on," she said, putting her arm through Eve's. "Let's go gorge ourselves on pasta."

Why did Maria have to be so damn friendly and nice?

"There's a look; I can always tell," Mrs. Spezia said, ignoring Eve's denial.

It was much later, and Eve had been helping clear up when she found herself alone in the kitchen with Maria's mother. There was no escaping the crafty woman's questions—and judgment.

"I been watching how you look at Vittorio when you think he doesn't notice. And he does the same thing, but not so sneaky. Men don't cover up so good as women."

"But Maria . . ."

"Another one!" Mrs. Spezia cried throwing up her hands. "Putting on such a show. Big tennis star. All smiles—when she wins. But inside it's different."

Eve's look was uncomprehending.

"My Marie is thirty-two years old. She should quit playing games and get married."

"If that's what Maria wants." What else could Eve say?

"You think she knows? One day it's this, the next day

that. But I know my daughter. It's time. Maria needs to settle down. But not," she leveled a sharp look at Eve, "not with Vittorio."

The blanket statement startled Eve.

Shaking her head for emphasis, Mrs. Spezia said, "He's not for her."

"They've been together for a long time."

The other woman pounced. "Exactly. That proves it. If it was meant to be, they should have gotten married long ago. I'm not saying they've got no feelings for each other, but it's like friends, or brother and sister. Eve, you can't cook a meal on a slow flame that keeps flickering on and off."

"Doesn't it say something that it *does* keep reviving?" asked Eve. Was she playing devil's advocate in hopes that her argument would be defeated?

"You know why? Because each feeds into the other's weakness."

Eve, who never thought of either Maria or Vic as weak, didn't understand.

"Maria, she's afraid of giving up being famous and running around the world playing tennis. Vittorio's afraid of being tied down," Mama explained. "So neither pushes the other to change. Now this Frazier Doyle, he's different." Mama gave a satisfied nod. "He's pushing. See how he looks at Maria? Like you look at Vittorio. There's just one thing wrong; he's not Italian," she said with a grin that elicited a like response from Eve. "Good . . . you're smiling. You'll see. It will all work out. I feel it in my bones."

"My bones must be on a different wave length," Eve said wryly.

"It's like this play I saw on Channel Thirteen last month, *A Comedy of Errors*. I thought it was maybe something with Steve Martin to make me laugh, but it was Shakespeare. That funny way of talking that's hard to understand. But you could see the mess these four people had got themselves into. Each one loved the wrong person, who finally turned out to be the right person for the other person. Crazy—huh? The good part is that it all gets fixed up in the end, and everybody's happy." Her smile broadened. She obviously expected the same kind of happy ending in the present scenario.

"Mrs. Spezia, that was a play written over three hundred years ago. There's no comparison. Whatever it is that keeps Vic and Maria together, maybe it's enough for them."

"You know that's not true."

"It's not for me to say."

With that final note, Eve ended the conversation by leaving the room. She spotted Vic and Maria in a corner in deep conversation. Frazier Doyle, across the room, was sitting on the arm of the couch laughing at something Tanya was telling him. Surveying the scene, Eve had to doubt Mrs. Spezia's interpretation of what was going on. Though she meant well, Maria's mother couldn't make something happen simply because she wished it. She couldn't control Maria's life.

But Eve could control her own, and she had every intention of doing so. Maybe Vic was ambivalent about his feelings. It was something only he could deal with.

Unless or until he did, Eve needed to distance herself from Victor Adesso. But how?

The opportunity unexpectedly came the following day.

Much too hot on deck, Glen claimed, so they sat in the lounge of *My Weakness* having a drink after their short cruise. The Avedons had enjoyed it, with Greta grudgingly admitting that Glen's boat was roomy, comfortable, and safe, "like a floating apartment". Which was probably why Eve wasn't enthusiastic. Not like the thrill of sailing on the *Hippolyta*.

Glen had been skillful at the wheel, easily guiding the twin-screwed boat past the other pleasure craft out on the

river. But not too considerate of smaller boats and sailboats, Eve had noticed, as he churned up a heavy wake
that bounced them about. She was glad to return to the
marina.

They were discussing what restaurant to choose for dinner when Bo sent a boy to summon Eve. "There's someone on the phone for you in the office. Bo said to hurry
'cause it's long distance," the youngster told her.

Probably from the Leonardtown neighbor who was looking after her house, Eve thought, hoping there was nothing
wrong. She rushed over and was surprised to see Vic on
the telephone. She gave Bo a questioning look.

"It's Al Fraser," Bo explained.

"From Montreal?"

"Yeah. He wanted to talk to Vic and to you."

"No. Everything's okay," Vic was saying. "She's
doing fine . . ."

Was he talking about Eve or the *Six Pack*?

"A five-day break, is it?" Vic said. "Well, you could
rent a runabout or something, couldn't you? . . . I see
. . . Hey, if I had the time, Al, I wouldn't mind sailing
up there and spending a few days tooling around Lake
Champlain with you . . . That's the way it goes. Yes,
she's right here."

He handed the phone to Eve just as Glen came through
the door with the Avedons.

Al Fraser said he just wanted to ask how Eve was managing. "Any problems?" he asked.

"No." *Not with the boat, anyway.* "I'm all settled in.
Everyone here's been very helpful."

Eve was listening to Al while trying to keep track of
the conversation going on in front of her. Glen was intro-
ducing Vic to "Eve's dear friends" and telling about their
river cruise. He was making it sound very cozy.

Then something Al Fraser was saying grabbed her attention. "So I have this five-day break between the two ses-

sions. If I'd thought of that earlier, I might have arranged to get the *Six Pack* up here instead of renting it out."

"Well, if that's what you want . . ." It would mean another stint of sleeping at the Avedons'.

"No, no. If you were a boating person, young lady, I'd pay your expenses to bring her up here and back, including a motel room on the lake. But of course, there's no way. I don't know why I even mentioned it."

Glen was talking about going to dinner. Had he asked Vic along? But no, he was just asking if Vic had any suggestions about where Glen should take the others. Vic shook his head and cast a cold look at Eve.

Eve and Fraser said good-bye, and she joined the others.

"Anything wrong?" Greta asked.

"No, except I feel kind of guilty. If I weren't living on the *Six Pack*, Dr. Fraser might have been able to get someone to take her up to Lake Champlain. If I knew how to run a boat . . ."

"Which you don't," Greta quickly reminded her.

Eve's mind was racing. "But maybe *I* could find someone to take me upriver. Someone here at the marina. I still have time before my class starts, and I could skip the first session if I had to. Bo, do you think—?"

Glen didn't let her finish. "Look no further, little lady." He took a little dancelike step and saluted. "Captain Rader at your disposal." He assured Eve that his antique and auction businesses could manage without him. "They usually do. I'm not around much during the summer anyway. I think that's a marvelous idea, Eve, doing old Fraser a good turn."

George looked dubious, Greta disapproving, and Vic grim. Eve probably looked the way she felt—confused and uncertain.

"That's ridiculous," Vic said.

"I don't think so at all." Glen turned from Vic to Eve. "What do you say?"

Vic didn't give her a chance to answer. "You've never gone all the way up the river, have you, Glen?"

"So what? I've cruised extensively."

"But not through the river locks."

"Look, old man, it doesn't take much navigational genius to tie up while the lockmaster changes the level of the water."

"Skill, not genius."

Glen was now irritated. "I've had power boats for years. Much larger, I might add, than Al Fraser's. In fact," he turned back to Eve, "I've an even better idea. We could make the trip on my boat, take *My Weakness* up there, turn her over to Al and borrow his car."

"I don't think I follow . . ." Eve began.

"It's simple; old Al would have the boat for five days, while you and I roam around the countryside, maybe run up to Quebec—"

Vic was glowering. "That's a bad idea."

His attitude was beginning to anger Eve. "Why?"

"For one thing, Al wants *his* boat, not Rader's."

Glen gave a supercilious laugh. "I should think he'd appreciate the substitution."

"You *should* think, but you usually don't," Vic shot back and turned to Eve. "It's a bad idea," he repeated.

"That's for me to decide."

"Then it's all set?" Glen asked.

"I didn't say that. I'll have to think about it."

Vic gave her a searing look, turned on his heels, and walked out.

At dinner, Eve tried to put that whole scene out of her mind. After all, dinner at Lutèce, the most expensive and elegant restaurant in New York, was a rare event. George was enjoying himself and even Greta was impressed. But for Eve, there was a fifth unseen presence at the table with them—Victor Adesso.

Vic had gotten so angry at Glen's proposal. Because he

doubted Glen's capability? Not likely. At least that wasn't the entire reason. His attitude had infuriated Eve, but she later questioned her reaction. She had resented his pronounced disapproval, but what if he'd voiced the opposite sentiment? Would she have preferred that Vic applaud her going off with Glen?

Mrs. Spezia was right. This was indeed like a comedy of errors—or a tragedy.

Eve needed to get away, to have time to think. Perhaps, from that point of view, going up to Lake Champlain was not a bad idea. Glen would need some tactful handling, but she was sure she could manage him, despite Vic's doubts. Could Vic possibly be jealous, or was that just wishful thinking on her part?

Becoming aware that the waiter was asking her a question, Eve smiled and nodded brightly. He promptly activated the large pepper mill he was holding and deposited a layer of black flecks on her salad.

Greta gave her a curious look. "I thought you didn't like pepper," she said.

Eve looked down at her plate and frowned. "I don't."

"Then why'd you tell him to put it on?"

"I didn't."

"You nodded Yes when the waiter asked," Greta told her.

Eve hadn't been paying attention. "A mistake."

This mistake was easily corrected. The waiter brought a new salad.

Too bad, Eve thought, that you couldn't make such easy exchanges all the time, just reverse a bad decision and start again. But some things, like how she felt about Vic, were irreversible. What she had to decide was what to do about it.

In the ladies' room after dinner, Greta asked, "You're not seriously thinking about that trip, Eve?"

They were sitting side by side in front of the mirrored wall. "I am. Very seriously."

Greta studied Eve's reflection. "Ahmm. I know that look. It's your 'keep your advice to yourself and don't mess with me' look."

Eve softened it with a small smile. "Something like that."

"Okay, okay." As they got up to go, Greta couldn't help asking, "So, you're going?"

"I'm going to sleep on it. I'll decide tomorrow."

In one sense, the decision was made for her. She awoke to the sounds of someone lumbering around on deck. Then Vic's call, "Eve, are you up?"

She scrambled out of bed, almost tripping on the sheet wrapped around her legs. Opening the cabin door, she peered outside. Vic had deposited a large cooler, a duffel bag, a tool box, and a lantern on the deck. "What are you doing?" she asked.

"What does it look like? We're taking the *Six Pack* up to Lake Champlain. Isn't that what you wanted?"

"Yes, but . . ."

"I'm going for a block of ice." He pointed to the hose on the dock. "You can fill the water tank. Oh . . ." He glanced at her nightgown, her tousled hair, "you'd better get dressed first." He stepped onto the dock and was gone.

Aghast, her mouth open, Eve stood there for a moment.

What did he think he was doing? Who did Victor Adesso think he was? What made him think he could just take over like this?

With such questions sputtering in her head, Eve went back inside. Operating on fast forward, she put away the bed linens, readjusted the dinette table, and zipped herself into one-piece denim romper shorts.

He'd be back in a minute, and then she would tell him. Tell him what? She could order him off the boat. And if he refused? Well, she could leave, just hoist herself ashore and wave good-bye.

Or—she could go with him.

Eve went out on deck just as Vic returned with a block of ice.

Pointing accusingly she started, "Now, look here . . ."

"In a minute. Let me get this into the icebox first."

When he came back out, he put his hands on his hips. "Okay, I'm looking," he said. "Not bad for a five-minute prep time. But you didn't comb your hair."

Her hand darted up to check, halted, then balled into a fist with frustration. "My appearance is not the point."

"What is?"

He sounded so damn reasonable. "Your highhandedness, for one," she sputtered.

"I'm sorry." Vic spread his hands in a conciliatory gesture. "You're right."

She looked closely for signs of sarcasm, but he seemed sincere. Somewhat mollified, she said, "We've got to talk."

"Sure." Vic sat on the stern seat. "Shoot."

"Not me. You shoot." Why did she have to sound so unnerved? "What makes you think you can come aboard without even a by your leave and take over? The *Six Pack* isn't your boat. It belongs to Dr. Fraser."

"Who gave me leave this morning to pilot her up to Lake Champlain."

"When this morning?" she asked suspiciously.

"I called him about an hour ago."

Eve was confused. "Why?"

"To ask how he'd feel about having Rader's boat up there." Vic inclined his head. "As I expected, he's not interested."

"If you remember," Eve pointed out tartly, "Glen first offered to take the *Six Pack*."

Vic shrugged. "Al vetoed that idea, too."

"Because you told him to."

"Maybe," Vic admitted, then added in a sterner tone, "It was an idea you should have voted against. Unless you want what he's offering."

Eve bristled. "Meaning . . . ?"

Vic's expression hardened. "Meaning I doubt the amorous Mr. Rader would be willing to sleep out here on deck."

"I can handle Glen Rader," Eve said with a toss of her head.

"Don't be so sure. Al and I agreed that I'd be the one to take the *Six Pack* up to him."

Eve's pulse skipped, then raced. She tried to slow her shallow breathing. "Didn't I hear you say you were too busy to take the time?"

"I'm making time."

He rested his elbows on his knees and leaned forward, fixing her with a hard expression. "Eve, if you want to go cruising with Rader on his boat, that's your business. But don't use Al Fraser as an excuse. Now, I'm taking this boat up north. If you want to come, that's fine, but I can't order you to . . ."

"Funny. I thought you were."

"You can pack some things," he said stiffly, "and stay on the *Hippolyta* until I get back."

Or on Glen's boat, she thought of saying.

Then, suddenly and quickly, Eve shed pretense. She had no desire to be with Glen Rader. Why taunt Vic, or herself? She had thought to get away from Vic to get her head together, decide what she wanted. But what she wanted was very clear. Vic! She was in love with him. It was *he* who had to make some decisions.

Perhaps time together, not time apart, was what they needed.

"I'll fill the water tank," Eve told him by way of her answer.

"Good," was all he said, allowing himself a slight smile.

Not a very ardent response, Eve thought. She sensed Vic's ambivalence, and cautioned herself to be ready for whatever happened.

Vic went forward to store some gear on the V bunks. "What's all this?" He pointed to the large box and her suitcase.

"I never unpacked all my clothes because there's not enough drawer or closet space. And that box has my sculpting stone and tools."

"How about I put this stuff on the *Hippolyta*? We need the space."

"All right."

"Anything you need from your suitcase?"

"No. I can make do with what I have."

"Good."

An hour later, they were on their way.

TEN

Vic's thoughts were indeed ambivalent as he guided the *Six Pack* out into the channel. Why had he told Al Fraser he would do this? He could have let Eve go with Rader. But Vic had to retract that lie immediately. The thought of Eve and Rader alone on the *Six Pack*, or on the larger boat, was insufferable. There was no doubt about Glen's motives. He would make his moves. Eve thought she could handle Rader, but the man had shown he had no scruples. Alone with him on a boat, Eve would be vulnerable. Vic found the idea abhorrent.

As for his own motives? Mixed.

Being near her was enough to flood him with desire and memories of their lovemaking. Visions of their afternoon together had been haunting him—Eve's naked loveliness, her abandonment in the throes of passion. She had been so greedy in her desire and so generous in gratifying his. He'd had satisfactory sex before. Often before. But not like this.

He and Maria had started out by being frank in what each wanted from the other. After all, this was the age of openness and free discussion. But this self-conscious approach lacked something essential, a spontaneity and naturalness flowing from an inner core. Eve's sexuality was a warm, glowing part of her, simultaneously pliant and passionate. His response was the same, emanating from deep within him.

Loving a woman like Eve, however, would require a complete change in the way he lived. Was he ready for that?

Vic wondered if Maria could have guessed that something had happened between him and Eve. The other night at her mother's house, they had talked for a while. Over the years they had never much indulged in heart-to-heart conversations. That night, Vic had the impression that they were both skirting around, not directly addressing what was on their minds.

What, after all, should he tell Maria? That he was drawn to another woman? That had happened before. That this one was different and special? But he didn't know just how important he could allow Eve to become in his life. And Maria obviously had been preoccupied with her own concerns. Even her elation over her tournament win had seemed strangely tempered. "So I won once more," she had said at one point. "What's next?"

His reply, "The U.S. Open, of course," hadn't really satisfied her.

"Yeah, I guess," she'd said and turned away.

Then this morning, when he had phoned her after talking to Al, Maria had sounded positively elated, urging him to make this trip, telling him to have a good time. "Eve's quite a gal," she had said. Meaning what?

He had admitted that Eve didn't yet know what he was planning. "She may not want to come along."

"Sure she will," Maria had said. "Don't go alone. It's not good to be alone."

She'd then mentioned her plans to drive up to New Hampshire for a few days' rest. He had offered her the Jag, but she'd declined. "Thanks, but I have a lift." Afterwards Vic had remembered that New Hampshire was where Frazier Doyle lived.

Now, thinking back on that conversation, Vic made up his mind to talk to Maria when he got back. Whatever happened with Eve, it was obvious that he and Maria had come to the end of the line. No sudden or traumatic shift. Though neither had wanted to acknowledge the fact, their relationship had changed. It had nothing to do with Eve, but she was the catalyst that was forcing Vic to examine and evaluate what was happening between him and Maria.

Fortunately, Maria wasn't the clinging type. Her career had always been the dominant love of her life. Hell, she could very well be reaching the same conclusions as he about calling a halt to their affair, though not, he hoped, to their friendship. He'd like them to remain friends. A civilized end to a long affair? Vic winced, and gave himself a mental jab. *Such a modern, rational, enlightened attitude!* Was he being a bastard, trying to excuse himself for moving from one woman to another?

It wasn't like that. Eve was not *another*, the next in line of a series of sexual partners. He'd never liked that game; he preferred a more long-lasting affair based on affection and respect as well as sex. But an affair was not a permanent commitment. From the very beginning, Vic had recognized that Eve played for keeps. If they had different expectations, it would be cruel to allow their intimacy to develop further.

For the time being, Vic felt he had no choice. He had insisted on protecting her from Glen Rader's advances. The inferred promise was that Eve would have nothing to fear from him. He intended to keep that promise.

How could Eve complain when Vic was being so scrupulously courteous—and maddeningly impersonal? When he wanted her to do something, he tacked a "please" on to his request. Except for that time they'd been pulling up to a gas dock and the *Six Pack*'s stern started veering sideways. Then he'd barked out an order. 'Eve, grab that friggin' pole. Fast.'' Leaning way out, she'd reached it and pulled the stern in. Later, he apologized. "I shouldn't have yelled like that.''

"It's okay." In fact, she could have added, I'd rather you yell than sound so friggin' polite.

She busied herself in the cabin for a time, until the lure of the river drew her to join Vic in the cockpit. It was a busy scene, different kinds of vessels going in all directions, from ugly barges to magnificent pleasure boats piloted by uniformed captains. Eve had to admire Vic's skill as he adjusted speed and altered direction when the need arose. He started to talk to her about the Hudson, and she realized how much he knew about the lore of the river and its history, how much he loved it.

"We almost turned this river into a giant sewer," he said bitterly at one point. "It's going to take a long time to clean it up, but at least we've made a start.''

At the upper end of Manhattan, they passed under the George Washington Bridge with its double-tiered span and never-ending stream of cars. Seen from this vantage point, it was beautiful, but Eve was glad she wasn't on it.

From here, the magnificence of the Palisades was breathtaking. Vic told her that there had once been talk of blasting them down for building stone. What a travesty that would have been. The high-rise apartment buildings along the top of the Palisades lessened, but couldn't destroy, their grandeur.

Farther on, the structures on the riverbanks ranged from historical mansions to cement factories. The skyline varied from smokestacks to treetops, according to the industrial or rural nature of the area. It was a constant panorama. For lunch, Eve made sandwiches which they ate while underway. Vic pointed out their location on the nautical chart and started to teach her about taking a bearing.

He even let Eve take the wheel for a little while, though he stayed close by. Across from Peekskill loomed the densely wooded Dunderberg Mountain. "Does the name mean what I think it does?" Eve asked.

"Sure does, because of the resident Dutch goblin responsible for whipping up summer thunder storms." Vic smiled. "There's all sorts of legends about this area."

There was a lot of pleasure-boat traffic around Bear Mountain and West Point. Too bad shore visits were out of the question. Vic must have read Eve's mind. "Maybe we can do a more leisurely return trip," he suggested. "Stop at some of these places. Would you like that?"

"I'd love it." She hoped she didn't sound too eager.

He gave her the wheel for another short spell that afternoon, but beyond Poughkeepsie, he took over again to maneuver around the rocks and shoals on the north side of Esopus Island. A short time later, he swung west into Roundout Creek. "We'll stay in Kingston for the night, okay?"

"Sure." As if she had a choice, Eve thought, but it was nice of him to ask.

They tied up at a large marina one mile up on the starboard side of the creek. Eve offered to cook dinner, but Vic said no. "It's been a long day. We'll eat out."

Out was a small Italian restaurant a half mile down the road. "Good, but not like Mrs. Spezia's," Eve said when they had finished their lasagna. "I don't know how Maria keeps her figure."

Vic's expression was a cross between a smile and a frown, but he said nothing.

Eve persisted. "Do you?"

"I never thought about it."

"But then she doesn't stay in Brooklyn much, does she?"

"I guess not." He got up to pay the check. The subject was closed.

It was apparent that Vic didn't want to talk about Maria. Was that a good sign, or bad?

Back on the *Six Pack*, Eve helped Vic make a bed for

himself on deck, using the foam mattresses from the V bunks. He then disappeared for a walk while Eve got ready to go to sleep. Hearing him return, she poked her head out. "You all right?" she asked.

"Fine."

"Need anything?"

"Nothing."

Eve's thoughts were grumbling ones.

That's your trouble, Vic Adesso. You don't need nothing from nobody. Or do all those negatives make a positive . . . meaning you do need something? What? Apparently not me.

Perhaps he no longer felt the same desire he'd had before—but Eve really didn't want to believe that. Vic had presented himself as a safe alternative to Glen Rader. He was probably determined to keep things between them on a strictly impersonal footing. By a supreme effort, she hoped. Why did he have to be so damn righteous? She wouldn't have wanted to fight him off, but a little tussle would have been flattering. She was ashamed at the thought. Having always detested flirtatious posturing, here she was craving to be wooed so she could say no.

But why was she kidding herself? She wouldn't say no. The truth be told, if Vic held out his arms, she would fly into them. If he told her he wanted her, his wish would echo her own.

Beyond Troy, they encountered the Troy lock, the first of a series they had to go through to get to Ticonderoga where Al Fraser was meeting them. The traffic was heavy. "What now?" Eve asked as Vic got into position behind a line of other boats.

"Nothing. We wait our turn to go in."

"And then?"

"The lock gets filled with enough water to raise us to the level of what's on the other side. About seventeen feet for this one, I think."

"And what do we do?" Eve wanted to know what to expect.

"Stay in position in the lock and keep the *Six Pack* from scraping against the side or ramming another boat. I put a fender board over the side, but there'll be some bobbing about, and you need to keep the bow from rubbing. That's what those poles are for." He'd taken out a long mop in addition to the boat hook.

He made it sound easy enough, but Eve was apprehensive. She didn't want to goof. Finally it was their turn. Vic handed her the mop and told her to go around to the forward deck. She was glad to have the railing to hang on to. Vic was powering forward very slowly, but the boat traffic made the water choppy and her footing unsteady. It was a tricky business. They motored into a canyonlike compartment. When the last boat entered, Eve heard the huge gate clank shut behind them.

Thank goodness I'm not claustrophobic, Eve thought nervously.

"Can you hear me?" Vic called.

"Yes," she yelled back with all the bravado she could muster.

"All you have to do is fend off and keep us from scraping, okay."

"Okay." Eve kept her eyes glued to the slimy black wall as Vic deftly eased the *Six Pack* into position on the left side and tied up.

Suddenly Vic hollered, "Eve, look to your starboard."

Starboard? Oh, God, which side was that? Why was he confusing her? But then she saw the bow of another boat drifting dangerously close on the right. Eve scrambled over, leaned far out, and held the other boat off until it pulled away.

Vaguely catching Vic's shout of, "Good girl," Eve blew out her breath in relief and went back to her job of keeping the *Six Pack* from rubbing against the wall. Once she got the hang of it, she relaxed enough to look around.

The water was boiling in to float the boats up to the level of the waterway ahead. There were eight other boats in the lock, and in almost every one, a woman was up in the bow while the man was in the cockpit.

When the water flow ceased and the doors on the other end opened, there was a roar of starting motors. Vic waited and took his place in the orderly line exiting the lock. There was one bad moment when a large powerboat in a hurry started jockeying past and cut in front of Vic. Eve, still forward, saw Vic mouthing inaudible curses. Her message was more eloquent. When the driver of the boat in front of them looked back, Eve used a gesture she'd never before tried.

When she rejoined Vic, he was smiling. "Good job," he said.

"I'm not sure I used the right finger."

He burst into laughter. She liked the sound, as open as the wind that carried it. "I didn't mean that," he said. "The whole thing." He put his hand on her shoulder, linking them. "You were great."

His praise sent a bubbling warmth through her chest. "So were you." She grinned. "Only next time, how about me in the cockpit and you fending off on the slippery forward deck?"

"You'd handle the lines, too?"

"Sure. Why not?"

His laughter surged again. "Am I being faced with a mutiny?"

"No. But why is the woman always the one with the mop?"

"Next time you can take the boat hook forward."

"That's not the point." It was a joking conversation on both their parts.

"No male chauvinism, intended . . . I swear it."

"So we switch?"

"Okay, but not quite yet. Perhaps when we're heading back downstream. I really think you should perfect your fending skills before advancing to the next level.'' A smile hovered around his mouth, and his eyes had sunny glints in their depths.

Eve didn't mind Vic's teasing, which was preferable to that earlier gentlemanly politeness. As he averted his glance to steer properly, Eve stepped closer, and Vic's hand dropped to her waist. Neither of them said anything, but Eve felt a flood of contentment.

The wind picked up toward later afternoon. There was little traffic, most of the pleasure boats having headed in. Eve had gone below for a minute when she felt the sudden change of course. ''What's up?'' she asked, coming on deck.

Vic pointed. ''That boat's in trouble.'' He picked up speed and headed for a small sailboat up ahead. The sail was down. ''Cracked mast,'' Vic muttered grimly. A teen-age girl was standing and waving desperately. As they came closer, Eve saw the man in the cockpit, clutching his right arm. Vic eased alongside and put his motor in neutral.

''My dad's hurt,'' the girl cried desperately.

''Got hit by the boom,'' the man called out. ''Broke my arm. Coulda rowed her in otherwise. I could use a tow.''

''You got it,'' Vic told him.

Obviously relieved, the man said, ''I shoulda been more careful. I feel like a damn fool.''

''Forget it. Things happen.''

In minutes, Vic had fastened a tow line to the sailboat and helped the girl and her father to board the *Six Pack* where they'd be more comfortable. Eve soothed the teen-ager while Vic deftly converted a pillowcase into a sling to immobilize the man's arm. Fortunately, they were close to the man's yacht club, where they surrendered the crippled sailboat and the grateful pair to waiting friends. After some hurried thank you's, Vic and Eve took off again.

Eve looked at her watch. "That whole thing took less than a half hour," she said with some wonderment.

"So?" he asked quizzically.

"You were pretty good."

He seemed genuinely surprised. "They needed help? What's the big deal?"

"Nothing."

Eve couldn't explain. She wasn't sure what had prompted her original decision to come with Vic, but something was happening on this trip. Perhaps she'd wanted to see what he was like when they were completely away from others, to make mental notes, positive and negative. And so where was she?

There was that stubborn streak of his, but it also held a dimension of strength. Strength, too, in his handling the boat—though anyone with experience might have done as well. In an emergency situation, he acted deftly and with authority, too.

More pluses than minuses, Eve thought, and had to laugh at herself. All the negative aspects seemed to have a positive side. Proving what—that Vic Adesso was a multifaceted human being. Heaven help her, she loved the man, not his attributes.

It was late in the afternoon when Vic decided that they'd done enough for the day. "We'll stop over at Cohoes on the west bank," he said.

"Whatever you say." It had been such a good day. Eve didn't want it to end.

"I remember a shipyard in the area. There should be a marina. Or . . ." he hesitated. "Or we could overnight on the hook."

"Come again?"

"On the hook translates to anchoring out. Instead of tying up to a dock as we did last night." His tone was casual, but there was a questioning intensity in his gaze that set her blood racing.

"Why not? I'm game for it," she said.

"It means no shore facilities," he warned.

"I know."

"No shower."

"I know." None of that mattered. What mattered was this clamoring inside her breast.

His voice took on a teasing tone. "And we'd have to cook on board."

"Are you trying to discourage me?"

With a wide, satisfied smile, Vic said, "Just want to be sure."

"I'm sure," she told him with soft conviction.

Vic had mentioned the difficulties, but Eve's mind fastened on only one thought. They would be truly alone.

The *Six Pack* became their own tiny island. They dropped anchor in a safe area near Cohoes. There were only three other boats moored there, and Vic was careful to anchor well away from them. So there'd be no problems as the boats swung on their anchors during the night, he explained. Eve understood the practical need and appreciated the privacy it afforded.

After he was satisfied that the anchor wasn't dragging and the boat was secure, Vic proposed a drink. "To celebrate your passing today's ordeal with flying colors."

"It wasn't that bad," Eve told him. "In fact, I kind of enjoyed the whole thing."

He cocked his head and gave her a speculative smile. "Yes, I think you did."

"But I'll have that drink anyway. After I wash up first." She held up grimy hands sore from pushing on mop handles and pulling on lines. Vic showed her the slimy residue on his hands and arms. There was also a smudge on his cheek where he must have rubbed it. "After we both wash up," she amended. "You're dirtier, so you first."

He finished quickly and poured their drinks while Eve scrubbed her face and hands. Catching a glimpse of herself in the mirror of the small medicine cabinet, she saw tan-

gled hair and a sunburned nose. A little makeup . . . ?
Nah! Vic was waiting.

On deck, he'd set up the small folding table he'd
thought to bring along. With their drinks, he had put out
crackers, a wedge of cheese, and an open can of smoked
oysters, all on paper plates.

"Hors d'oeuvres? Great," she said.

"Not exactly elegant, but the best I could do. I warned
you about roughing it."

Eve sat on the seat next to Vic. "Who needs elegant?
Not the way I look."

"You look fine."

"With my sunburned nose?"

"And shoulders." His large hand on her shoulder was
cooling to her reddened skin, but had the opposite effect
internally. Did he sense her reaction? Vic's hand tightened, then dropped away.

He gave her her drink. "Some more of Al's brandy."

"Brandy's for after dinner."

"Okay. After dinner we'll do it again. We'll have to
buy him a replacement bottle," he said.

"Yes, we will." Eve liked using the plural pronoun.

Vic clinked her glass. "Here's to today."

"And tomorrow," she added softly.

Over the rim of his glass, his eyes held hers. He drank
deeply. "Tomorrow should be an easier day," he said,
picking up on only the surface meaning of her toast. "Unless the wind kicks up. The last boating forecast wasn't
clear. If it's bad, we might have to hole up for a day."

"Here?" Eve didn't say that she wouldn't mind at all.

"No. We'd have to put into a marina."

Shrugging, she said jauntily, "If we have to, we have
to."

Eve took a cracker, topped it with cheese, ate it, and
immediately took another. "I didn't realize how hungry I
was. Dig in before I eat it all."

Vic smiled at her. "You're proving me wrong, you know."

She cocked her head. Through a mouthful of crackers she asked, "How so?"

"My first impression that day I saw you tripping down the dock . . . helpless female."

She swallowed her mouthful and grinned. "Well, that day I sure felt like a novice. Hell, I *was* a novice when it came to living on a boat. But not a helpless female," she added with spirit. "Never that. There is a difference, you know. A novice can learn. It's a temporary state."

"I stand corrected."

They sat companionably, talking a little, drinking, munching on crackers and cheese. Eve put the last two oysters on a cracker, then licked the oil off her fingers. "See, now I couldn't do this if we were being elegant, could I?"

"Why not? You're always doing things that surprise me."

"Is that good?"

He reached out, his fingers lightly caressing her face. "I'm not sure," he said.

Eve caught her breath. This merest touch could send her blood racing hotly through her. His hand dropped away. The moment passed and she breathed again.

Striving for a casual tone, Eve asked, "Want half of this?" She held out the cracker.

"Since it's the last one . . ." He guided her hand to his mouth and bit off half. She popped the rest into her mouth. A playful exchange, but with a sensual undertone.

Eve waited, wondering if Vic would pick up on it. He didn't.

She stood up. "Well, my next surprise is going to be the gourmet dinner I'm about to prepare on that two-burner galley stove."

"Gourmet? I'll settle for filling."

"You'll see."

She took him up on his offer to help. Vic cut up the salad ingredients while Eve took care of the main course. They kept bumping into each other in the tight quarters. Conversation came easily, with no special focus or topic. Vic described the time he'd taken off with his father's boat and run aground in Long Island Sound. Eve remembered a backcountry camping trip with college friends when a bear got into their food. Just trading stories. But Eve felt their growing closeness.

"*Violà*," she said with a flourish as she set their dinner plates on the dinette table. "Tender nuggets of chicken in a creamed mushroom sauce, rice pilaf, and baby carrots. See what an imaginative cook can do with a few cans and a package of rice?"

"Hey, don't forget my contribution." Vic centered the salad bowl on the table. "Salade à la Vic with my own superb vinaigrette dressing."

"The true test is in the eating," Eve told him.

"So let's do it."

Their dinner passed the test.

Eve refused Vic's offer to clean up afterward. Using disposables meant there was little to do. But she was glad he stayed seated at the dinette table while she washed the cutlery and a couple of pots and put things away. She was drying the last fork when Vic stood and came up behind her.

"I'll put on the coffee," he offered. "Where do you keep the percolator?"

She turned and he was so close, physically filling all the space around her. Eve was aware of the rise and fall of his chest as he breathed, the musculature of shoulders and arms, the smokiness of his eyes, and the strong contours of his face. As she gazed at him, his expression seemed to tighten.

"You missed a smudge," she said. Vic gave an involuntary start as her fingers touched his cheek. "It's just a little dirt." Eve rubbed it away.

Vic took her hand and brought it to his lips. It was in that second that something seemed to change in him. Their eyes met and held for a long moment, a moment of affirmation.

Then he smiled, dropped her hand, and proceeded to put on the coffee. They brought their steaming mugs outside so they could watch the sun take its final plunge. The sky was magnificently multihued, with sweeping ribbons of color from orange to mauve unfurling across the sky.

They didn't speak. With Vic's arm around her, Eve rested back, her head nestled into the depression just below his shoulder. A hot wind sent the *Six Pack* drifting in a circular pattern around its anchor, giving them a constantly changing panorama of sky and shore and water. Sounds of boats still plying their way through the main channel seemed far away. Eve caught occasional glimpses of people on the other three boats, but the voices barely carried, like whispers on the wind. Or was the powerful drumming of her heart drowning out all other sounds?

She uttered a protesting murmur when Vic rose. "I'll just be a minute," he promised. "We need an anchor light so no one smacks into us." She noticed that the other boats were also thus lighted. Vic returned quickly, and she settled back against him with a contented sigh.

The sun was gone now, leaving behind an auburn glow that resisted the darkness. But only for a while, until it was absorbed by enveloping night.

"Day's end," Vic said softly.

"Hmm." Eve moved her head slightly to better pick up his chest vibrations when he spoke. "Not really an ending . . . just part of a continuing cycle."

His lips against her hair, Vic asked, "Wouldn't you like to have constant daylight, white nights, like in the far north?"

"Oh, no. I love evening, and the half dusk like now. When harsh outlines blur, like the boat over there, and then slip into shadow."

"And then blackness."

"But there are stars. Look, you can begin to see them. And that sliver of moon up there." She stared into the sky. "You know, I'm kind of sorry that a man actually stepped there."

"You mean you wouldn't want to walk on the moon?" His voice was low and teasing.

"No. I'm right where I want to be."

Eve realized how true that was. They were completely isolated, she and Vic, on this small boat. For now, it was the only place in the world, and Vic was the only person who mattered. *I love you*, Vic, she thought, *completely and forever*.

His hand slid to her waist, then up to her breast. Eve placed her hand over his, pressing it against her, following his circular caresses. The pleasant warmth in her body began to flow to a central burning core. "Eve," Vic whispered. She swiveled to face him, her lips parting to welcome his kiss. In its very tenderness, Vic's kiss was more demanding than any she'd ever known, seeking to draw from the depths of her—everything—all she had to give.

ELEVEN

Vic stood, drawing Eve with him, clinging to her lips. She didn't need the pressure of his arms to bend her body to him. It responded to her own need, pressing closer, moving against him, welcoming his mounting excitement and matching it with her own. She put her arms up, rising on bare toes and clasping her hands around his neck. Vic raised his head and spoke her name again . . . questioning. Eve's smile of assent was the answer he craved.

Vic took the foam cushions from the seats to fashion a bed for them right where they stood, then kneeled, pulling her next to him. He drew her shirt over her head, undid her bra, peeled off his shirt and enfolded her in his arms. His kiss promised what her heart longed for and her body craved. Eve felt an inner tightening as her breasts rubbed against the grating roughness of his bare chest. Her fingers delighted in the heat and strength of his torso, the muscular tension under his skin. She reveled in all the tantalizing sensations.

Vic's mouth, moist and seeking, traveled to her ear, where his tongue explored the crevices, creating shivering darts of pleasure that ran through her bloodstream. His hands moved caressingly down her back, around her waist, and to the fullness of her breasts. His mouth dropped to the pulsating hollow of her throat. Eve arched back and Vic took up the silent invitation. He bent his head to her breasts, kissing, caressing, his tongue circling, his mouth gently tugging, fulfilling her need for this touch while arousing a further aching.

Vic lifted her legs and bent her back onto the cushions. She raised her hips to help him take her jeans off. With deliberate slowness, he did the same with the lacy panties, letting his fingers trail tantalizingly over her bare skin as he eased them over her hips and thighs and legs. In seconds, he'd stripped and stretched out beside her.

The sides of the boat shielded them from view. Except from above, where the stars, stark against the now black sky, witnessed with passion.

How beautiful she was, Vic thought, her nude body softly outlined by starlight. Vic's doubts and reservations had drowned in the tide of tenderness and desire that overwhelmed him. He wanted to prolong this lovemaking, postponing final release to savor all the nuances, to provoke and indulge Eve's every desire.

He kept apart from her at first as his hands began their sensuous exploration. He traced patterns on her breasts, spanned her waist, and stroked from her slender hips down her outer thighs and legs and toes, then traced another trail upward to her quivering inner thighs, through the dark brush of curls to her navel and back to the thrusting peaks of her breasts. He made his fingers instruments of delight for both of them, smoothing and kneading and probing.

He moved closer so that his mouth and lips and tongue could trace the same paths, made even more tantalizing by Eve's tremulous, heightened sensitivity and soft moans of pleasure. But soon she was no longer content to let him lead. Eve reached for him, hesitatingly at first, but then with growing ardor. She kissed his mouth and eyes and face, and her tongue flicked a fiery code into his ear. He tried to lie still, allowing her passion full rein. Eve's hands teased with tentative prodding, glided over the hard contours of his chest, the dipping plane of his belly, and made daring forays below, threatening his endurance. With a gasp of delight at her boldness, he watched Eve straddle him. She trailed a series of kisses from his eyes to the hollowed center of his throat, and then stretched out on top of him.

"Vic, please," she whispered, and he exulted at her desire and readiness. He raised her to position himself against her, then eased himself into her. She cried out, and for a second Vic feared she would draw back. But she didn't. The cry softened to a murmur and she pressed down to allow for deeper penetration. He kept his body still, just holding her close, until he sensed her tightening around him and he could begin his delving search for the center of her passion and the source of his.

Eve, being above him, could set the pace. She did, relishing what appeared to be an unaccustomed freedom for her. She dipped and rose rhythmically, accommodating him, pushing more deeply into his thrust. She arched back, and he marveled at the beauty of her body, the look of abandoned joy on her face. Vic pushed himself up to kiss her breasts and pull her against his chest. He felt the urgency tightening deep inside her, and his imminent pounding through to reach it.

Never before had he been so aware of this moment before orgasm. Instead of hurtling toward release, Vic was acutely tuned in to Eve's feelings as well as his own. He rolled her onto her back and held himself over her, quickening his movements in response to her inner writhing. He felt her tighten, then lock around him. His mouth stifled her cry as her hips rocked violently and he thrust down into the shuddering softness.

They lay locked together as passion ebbed from their bodies. Vic then eased himself to her side and held her close. It was a new experience for him, the outpouring of love that Eve had just shown. He felt her shiver. The night air was beginning to chill bodies no longer warmed with desire. "Shall I get a blanket," he asked, "or would you rather go inside?"

"The blanket," she whispered. "Let's sleep under the stars."

He brought out pillows, too. Eve burrowed in close to him and sighed sleepily. Just as she closed her eyes, he whispered, "I love you, Eve."

In the early morning, a violent rocking woke them.

"What in hell?" Vic started, sat up, and peered around. "Damn fool," he said.

Eve raised onto one elbow. "What's up?"

"A damn fool is up and away." He pointed to a departing power boat whose turbulent wake was shaking the *Six Pack.* "One of our neighbors determined to get an early start."

Eve pulled Vic's arm. "We don't have to be damn fools, too, do we?"

"The damn fool part was because of his speed, not his timing." He looked at his watch. "It's six-thirty. The sun'll be up soon."

But it was still gray and misty. "We watched the stars come out from here. Why not watch the sun come up?" Eve gave him what she hoped was a captivating smile.

His was suspicious. "Are you trying to seduce me?"

She gazed at him through narrowed eyes. Even in the predawn grayness, his skin had a tawny sheen, and his dark hair fell over his forehead. She remembered running her fingers through his hair, over his body. "Now that you mention it . . ."

His laugh was low and excitingly suggestive. He slid back under the blanket and pulled her to him. An inner stirring made her tremble.

"Are you cold?" His lips were against her ear.

"Quite the contrary," was her soft reply. "How about you?"

"Need you ask?"

Feeling the heat of his arousal against her, she shook her head.

This time they came together quickly and joyously, sure of the other's response and gratification. They teased and laughed in a lusty joining. Different from last night's prolonged foreplay, Eve thought afterward, but still deeply felt—and fun. With Vic, sex would never become routine.

"I feel the sun on my back," Vic told her. "You missed the sunrise."

"Because you blocked my view."

"Complaining?"

"No." She trailed a finger down his chest. "There'll be another one tomorrow."

"And the day after that, and after that . . ."

But how far into the future? Vic kissed her tenderly and made a move to get up. "Vic, wait." He turned back. "Last night, before I slept, I thought I heard . . . maybe it was in a dream . . . you said . . ."

"What?"

" 'I love you.' " Her voice was barely a whisper.

He shook his head in refutation; Eve's heart fell.

"It was no dream," he said.

So it wasn't a denial.

"I said it, and I meant it."

Past tense? "In the throes of passion?" she had to ask. Men often made empty declarations of love during sex.

"*After* the throes of passion, if my memory serves," he said. He took her chin and tilted her head up. "Though it could have been before or during. Maybe I said it again as you slept, or in my dreams."

Her heart swelled at the message in his eyes, but she yearned to hear it once more. "Say it now, please."

"I think it's your turn."

Eve was happy to give words to her silent avowal. "I

love you, Victor Adesso. I think I have from the very beginning, and I'll love you forever.''

His look was jubilant, but his question teasing. ''Will a 'me, too' suffice?''

''No way.''

''Okay. God knows I tried not to complicate my life, but there it is. I love you.''

The sound of a motor revving up caught his attention. ''We better get dressed before someone alerts the Coast Guard that there are a couple of indecently exposed characters floating around here. Come on.'' He draped the blanket to shield them as they went below.

A modest sponge bath was the best they could do. They were still kind of grungy, but they were grungy together. The day was warming up as the sun rose higher so she put on white cotton sheeting shorts and a loose T-shirt decorated with a SAVE THE SNOW OWL logo.

''I didn't know you were into owls,'' Vic said.

''I'm into protecting all endangered species,'' she told him.

He shook his head and grinned. ''That, too? How much more don't I know about you?''

''Lots. But you'll have plenty of time to find out.'' *Like a lifetime?* But she didn't say the words, afraid of tempting fate by counting on too much.

Vic studied his charts and listened to the marine weather channel while Eve made coffee and scrambled eggs. Something gnawed at her. Vic had said he loved her, but there was that part about not wanting to complicate his life. She brought it up during breakfast.

''I don't mean to complicate your life.''

''With scrambled eggs? No problem. Now something fancy like Eggs Benedict, that's another story.''

He was treating her concern as a joke. ''Vic, be serious.''

''Okay. Truth is, you can't help but complicate my life,'' Vic said. ''Eve, don't look at me that way. It's not an accusation, just a statement. Complication goes with the territory. Things have to change . . ." He frowned as he broke off what he was saying.

"You're thinking of Maria?"

"That's one thing," he admitted.

"You loved her?"

"We've been lovers. I told you that." He pushed away his plate. Both had forgotten about eating.

"So there's an obligation?"

"I'm not trying to deny it. But what kind of obligation?"

The frustration in his tone suggested that he'd been puzzling over this question.

"We had something going for a long time," he continued, "but circumstances change. People change. I think Maria and I hung on together out of habit. And there was no special draw elsewhere—until that day you came tripping into my life." He reached across the table and took her hand. "Maria deserves honesty. She wouldn't want a man who loves someone else."

Remembering Mrs. Spezia's prediction, Eve wanted to believe that Vic was right. But the beautiful tennis star had a volatile personality. She was used to claiming Vic when she wanted him.

"Are you still sleeping with her?" His expression showed frowning surprise, but Eve forged ahead. "Like that night when she came to see you on the *Hippolyta*?"

In measured tones, he replied, "I have not been with Maria, or anyone else, since I met you two weeks ago."

Two weeks? Had it been such a short time since she'd come to New York? So much had happened. "And before that?" she asked.

He took a last gulp of coffee and got up. "Before that was before you," he said with finality.

"Oh." What kind of answer did she expect? An enumeration? Of course, Vic must have had many sexual experiences, but Eve clung to the belief that he'd never before given himself so completely as he had to her. Before stepping outside, he turned and gave her a broad smile, a confident smile. She read in it that he would work things out; all would be well. It was the message she wanted.

"Ready for your next gig as first mate?" Vic asked.

She saluted smartly. "Ready and able."

"Then let's get under way."

It was an idyllic day, Eve thought. At Waterford they got into the narrow, winding Champlain Canal system which would lead to the open waters of Lake Champlain sixty miles to the north. The transit of four more locks took a long time. Not so much running time as waiting to be admitted to each one, making fast in the lock, waiting for the water depth to change, and then the slow filing out.

Eve adeptly handled her part of the process. Determined to hold Vic to his promise to change places on the return home, she also studied what he was doing. After choosing his spot inside, Vic tended the lines which held the *Six Pack* to its position against the wall, taking the lines in as the boat rose. It would be the other way around on the return trip.

In one of the smaller locks, the *Six Pack* was the last to enter, and there was little room left against the walls. Vic was about to squeeze into a marginally adequate space when a ruddy-faced man on a forty-foot cruiser called to him, "Hey, don't sweat it. You can raft up with me."

"Okay, thanks," Vic replied.

Eve, ready to take her place forward, paused to ask, "What's rafting up?"

"We're going to tie up to this other boat."

"How?"

"You'll see." Vic wasn't into explaining at the moment. He tossed her one of the fenders used to protect the sides. "Tie this on that middle cleat and put it over the side. Then this other one on that aft cleat. And get ready to toss the bow line.''

Eve followed orders quickly, with little wasted motion. In less than three minutes, she was standing forward with the bow line as Vic slowly guided their boat forward. *If Greta could see me now*, she thought, laughing to herself. Two weeks ago, she would never have dreamed she'd be scrambling around doing chores on a boat headed upriver. Her face was sunburned, her clothes wrinkled and damp, her hands sore, but Eve would not have traded this experience for anything.

She noticed the name in gold script on the stern of the boat ahead, CATHY D, from Yonkers. A slender woman with straight black hair and a toothy grin was on the forward deck. Her short shorts showed off a shapely pair of legs. As Vic came abreast, he cut the motor and told Eve to throw her line to the other woman. In minutes, the two boats were rafted together. Invited to come aboard, Eve and Vic climbed over onto the other boat. Eve went forward to help fend off, but there was little need. The *Cathy D*'s fender board was a monstrous and very efficient protection.

"Hi. I'm Eve Marsdon. You must be Cathy D.''

"Nope. Sally Ann Dreher.'' Sally Ann flashed that toothy smile again. "Cathy was Art's second wife. Lasted nine months. We only been married since December. Art says we gotta go to one year before he pays for a new name.'' She laughed. "Just to be sure he's not wasting his money.''

Eve was curious. "That doesn't bother you?''

"Nah. Ain't he a pisser?''

It was said admiringly. Eve had to laugh. "Think you'll make it?'' she asked.

"Sure. How about you? That's one handsome hunk you got yourself. How long you been married?''

"We're not.''

Sally Ann pursed her lips and raised her eyebrows. "Oooh, you mean he's available?"

"Nooo. I didn't say that."

Sally Ann gave a good-natured shrug. "I gotcha." She leaned over to glimpse Vic talking to her husband, a tall man with a wide girth around the middle. Her comparison over, she turned back to Eve. "Hey, they're the same height, and flat bellies ain't such a big deal. But if I was you, Eve, I'd tie that guy up real fast."

Unfortunate terminology, Eve thought, though the other woman obviously meant well. Vic was not a man to be tied up.

"The ring and the license, honey. That's what it's all about." Sally Ann added.

By the time Eve and Vic had a fast tour of the *Cathy D*'s comfortable and roomy interior, the outer gate of the lock was about to open. They returned to the *Six Pack*, undid the connecting lines, and waved good-bye to Drehers.

"The *Cathy D*'s a nice cruising boat," Vic commented.

"Yes, it is." Eve took in the fenders and wound up the line, looping it around her elbow as she'd seen Vic do and storing it away.

"Envious?"

"No," she answered truthfully. "I've become quite attached to our boat."

He laughed. "You mean Al Fraser's boat, don't you?"

"Of course." But for now, it belonged to her and Vic.

"Someday we'll do this cruise on the *Hippolyta*, maybe sail all the way to Canada," Vic said. He caught her expression. "What's the matter? Don't you want to?"

"I do. I just couldn't help thinking of Loretta's boat, how she and her husband named it *Someday*, but their day never came."

"Too much planning ahead. Sometimes it keeps you from making the most of what you have right now." His smile reminded her that they still had the present.

"When will we get to Ticonderoga?" Eve asked.

"Late tomorrow, if all goes well."

Eve wished it were longer. She told herself it didn't matter; she and Vic would have time ashore together and then another homebound journey downriver. But she felt suddenly apprehensive. On this boat right now, alone with Vic, they were insulated from the world. Here they could close out everything and everyone. But what about later on?

Eve was annoyed at herself for placing any importance on Sally Ann's admonition about the ring and the license. The woman didn't know her or Vic, and her flip comments had no relevance. Still, Eve became pensive as she went about her chores. There had been no mention of marriage; she and Vic had talked about love, but not marriage.

Social and sexual mores had changed, but Eve had grown up with small-town traditions; in her mind, love and marriage were linked. But that might not be the case with Vic. Until now he had avoided any permanent and legal tie. That word again. Perhaps Vic thought of marriage in a negative way. He'd implied that his parents had not been happy together. After his mother's death, Vic's father hadn't remarried, preferring to find companionship with a string of lady friends. Vic apparently hadn't minded. He'd admired and loved his father.

As a counselor, Eve was aware that people often unconsciously emulated the parent they most identified with.

Vic broke into her reverie. "Daydreaming?"

"Kind of."

"What about?"'

Not wanting to voice her doubts, all she said was, "Nothing special."

Take each day as it comes, she told herself. Time enough when they returned to New York to work out the complications that Vic had predicted. It goes with the territory, he'd said. But for now, their territory was here on the *Six Pack*, inviolate and safe.

"We'll stop near Schuylerville tonight," Vic told her.

"On the hook?"

He grinned. "No, not on the hook."

She was disappointed. "Why not?"

"Because we have to gas up, and we need ice and some provisions. And a shower."

"We can take sponge baths."

Vic shook his head. "We've also got to refill the water tank."

"So we'll conserve . . ." she coaxed. "Use a bucket of river water to wash."

"Take another look over the side." Vic pointed at some debris floating past. "The Hudson's still a long way from being sanitary enough for your personal cleanup."

She threw out her hands. "We can stay smelly and grungy for one more day."

"I don't know about that," said Vic with a grin. "I've never slept with a smelly, grungy woman."

He had a point. "Okay. You win."

"Good. Besides, we don't want to look like a couple of derelicts when we meet up with Al."

Another point.

Near Schuylerville, Vic took an eastern inlet and pulled into a small marina. Radioing ahead, Vic had gotten a slip assignment and they tied up at the end of one of the piers. While Vic was busy with the boat, Eve took toilet articles, a towel, and robe and headed for the shower room. The women's shower was a four-by-four alcove off the bathroom, not half as nice as at her marina. *Her* marina? Eve laughed to herself.

She stripped off her shorts, top, and undergarments, dropping them into a heap on the wooden bench outside the shower. Talk about grimy . . . And she was just as bad as those clothes. But not for long. Eve stepped into the shower, turned it on full blast, and gave herself a good scrubbing.

Afterward she scrutinized herself in the mirror above

the wash basin and was satisfied. She glowed with cleanliness. Vic would not be sleeping with a grungy woman tonight. Eve felt a shiver of excitement. She put her hands to her breasts, pressing against the now-sensitive peaks.

My God, she thought, just the idea of being with Vic was enough to arouse her. She had never expected to feel this way again. But it was not really *again*, for she had never felt like this, not even with Graham, so acutely responsive physically, brimming with love and desire. Vic had tapped into a vibrant sexuality stronger than she'd ever experienced.

Eve put on her robe, gathered up her things, and headed back. Stepping onto the dock leading to their slip, she spied a boat with the same lines as the *Six Pack* pulling out.

It *was* the *Six Pack*.

Eve ran down the dock. "Hey," she yelled. But he didn't hear.

What in the world was happening? Where was Vic going? Had he left her behind? This was crazy. Here she was screaming and waving, standing on a dock someplace up north in New York State, clad only in a robe and flipflops, holding an armful of dirty clothes, watching the man she loved disappear into the sunset.

But he wasn't disappearing. Vic made a sharp right turn and headed in. Of course! Eve shook her head with relief and embarrassment. He was going in for gas. She turned back and was waiting to take his line as he pulled into the gas dock.

"Hi," he said with a grin. "Fancy meeting you here."

"You could have told me," she said, countering her embarrassment with anger.

"What?" His concern seemed genuine.

"Where you were going. I saw you pulling out and I thought—"

Grasping her meaning, he started to laugh. "Don't tell me you thought I was leaving you stranded?"

It *was* ridiculous, Eve realized, and laughed with him. How could she think that? Was it the uncertainty she tried to bury surfacing in such a wild notion?

Vic took her hands and pulled her toward him. "I would never do that," he said, continuing to tease, "especially now that you're so nice and scrubbed and squeaky clean."

"Not like someone I know," she countered, falling in with his light tone.

"That will soon be remedied. As soon as I gas up, I'm going to clean up to be worthy of you. Then I'll buy you the best dinner this town can offer. After which, we'll take our squeaky-clean bodies to bed. How does that sound to you?"

"Just fine."

"I especially like the 'after which' part."

Eve did, too.

The best dinner turned out to be nothing better than pizza and beer at a nearby tavern. But the 'after which' met all their expectations—and then some.

Eve hated to have the night end.

_____ TWELVE _____

So much for good intentions, Vic thought. His plan to be off at the crack of dawn didn't work out. They'd slept inside last night, crowded into the cabin berth, but neither had complained, even though the narrow accommodation, he remembered with a smile, had made for some interesting physical adjustments as they made love.

He'd awakened to find Eve stretching languorously beside him, the sheet around her hips, her upper body temptingly exposed. She saw he was up and twisted to face him. The sheet crumpled between them, and she pulled it away. The sleepiness in her green eyes gave way to sharp awareness. All she'd said was a soft "Hi there," but it was a heady invitation Vic couldn't resist.

So they were leaving a half hour later than he'd planned.

"What are you smiling at?" asked Eve as she joined him at the wheel.

"Nothing much. Just thinking about priorities."

"I hope I'm on your list."

"You are."

"High on the list?"

"Very high." He planted a kiss on her nose. "Now sit here and help me steer." He liked having her close.

Eve took the pilot's seat. Standing beside her, his arm around her shoulders, Vic knew that she'd become more than a priority. Priorities implied a freedom to choose, but he didn't seem to be able to exercise that kind of freedom with this woman. Not anymore. Eve had become a necessary part of him. The consuming physical attraction was an outer sign of something far deeper. And he had allowed it to happen.

With her complicity, he thought, remembering how completely she gave herself to their lovemaking.

"You've got that grin again," Eve accused.

"Just thinking of all the nice memories we're making. Not at all what I'd anticipated when we started out."

"What did you anticipate?"

"A chaste voyage with a bristly first mate, not a seductive temptress."

"Hold on there, Vic Adesso." Eve whirled around to confront him. "I did not try to seduce you."

"You don't have to try," he countered. "It just happened."

"It's not as though I set out to break your resolve . . ."

Vic realized that Eve was serious. His joking had upset her. "Eve, I was teasing. You didn't break my resolve—
I did. I take full responsibility, okay? Now smile."

She complied. Apparently mollified, Eve turned back to her steering.

During the course of the morning, however, Vic sometimes caught her with a pensive expression. He'd begun to sense what was on Eve's mind and knew she was apprehensive about the future. Vic had always thought of long-range planning as a technique reserved for business enterprises, preferring to keep his personal life spontaneous and unencumbered. His concerns were the immediate future—today, tonight, tomorrow, this weekend.

That would probably have to change. But not yet.

He put his mind to today's business, getting the *Six Pack* up to Ticonderoga with another seven locks to go. The next two locks posed no problems. The canal rejoined the Hudson below Billings Island.

Vic had been concentrating on navigating through the channel when he suddenly smelled something. His eyes immediately went to the engine compartment. Dammit! It looked like a thin spiral of smoke seeping through. He cut the engine at once.

Eve had been below preparing sandwiches for lunch. "Why are we stopping?" she called from the door opening.

"Eve, get forward."

"What's up?"

"I said, get forward." This time he shouted, and she started to move. If there was an explosion, she would be safer at the front of the boat.

Vic got to the stern, crouched on the back bench, and bent over the engine compartment. There was still a slender sliver of smoke leaking out. He leaned back on his heels and, with arms extended, gingerly lifted the cover. Several more barely discernible wisps escaped, but that was all. Suddenly he became aware of Eve coming up behind him.

"Do you need this?" she asked.

Her voice was strained, but her face was rigid with determination. She held out the fire extinguisher she'd gotten from the galley. Vic took it from her and turned back to examine the engine. But there was nothing to extinguish. Puzzled, he put it down and continued to search and probe. What the hell had caused the smoke?

"We're drifting," he heard Eve say. There was little enough traffic where they were, so Vic didn't react. A few minutes later, he heard the sound of the anchor hitting the water. Turning, he saw Eve at the bow, letting out the anchor line.

Good girl, he thought, and went back to scrutinizing the engine.

A half hour later, with still no clue, Vic decided that this was probably one of those flukes that happened occasionally. Something sparks for a second and that's it.

Despite Eve's protests, this time he made her go forward while he started the engine. No problem. He let it idle while he checked again to see if anything looked suspicious. Still nothing. So he called to Eve to pull up the anchor and they were on their way again.

It was only after he'd put in at a boat yard at Fort Edward and had the engine checked that Vic relaxed. There was nothing wrong. "It happens," the mechanic said with a shrug. Vic felt his tension drain away. He gave Eve a hug, then went to the office to pay his bill. When he returned, Eve had lunch waiting.

"I thought we'd eat here before starting out again," she said.

"When did you do all this?"

"It's just sandwiches and coffee. I was about to bring them out when you started making like Captain Bligh, bellowing at me to get forward."

Vic grabbed her by the elbows. "And you disobeyed, didn't you?"

"Damn right. If we go down, we go down together." She was joking, but the memory of danger clouded her eyes.

"I wanted you to get clear, just in case." Vic said.

"And what if you'd needed that fire extinguisher?"

She was right. He should have had the presence of mind to get it himself, but he'd been gripped by the imperative of protecting Eve. "There I goofed," he admitted. "But you didn't." He drew her closer. "You thought of the extinguisher, the anchor. You were great."

Her eyes crinkled. "I was, wasn't I? See how wrong you were about that 'helpless female' first impression?"

"I do indeed."

"But I wasn't wrong about you." She caught him around the neck, stood on tiptoe, and gave him a resounding kiss. "Vic Adesso, you are one helluva guy."

He lifted her off her feet and whirled her around.

They had a witness; the mechanic had come back with Vic's receipt. "Ain't love grand?" the man said with a knowing wink.

Neither Vic nor Eve was of a mind to dispute him.

After leaving Fort Edward, the canal became a narrow landcut. As they came upon lock nine in the system, Vic warned her that this was the first of the locks that would lower them to the level of Lake Champlain. "It's the same principle, only in the opposite direction."

It was a different feeling, however, as water rushed out of the lock and the boat sank down. Eve watched Vic paying out the line and wondered what would happen if it got snubbed around the post. She put the thought out of her mind and tended to her business of fending off. All went well, but as they filed out of the lock, Eve mentioned her dire thoughts.

"What if the line somehow got snagged up there and you couldn't pay out the slack? Would we just hang there against the side of the lock?"

"Hardly." He was laughing. "The line would probably break."

"Oh, great! So we'd end up in the drink."

"No." He decided not to tease her. "The lockmaster can flip a switch, stop the release of water, unsnag the line, and then start up again. There's no real danger."

"I'm glad to hear it."

"Come sit by me." Vic made room on the seat with him. He gave her a reassuring hug. "You can relax," he told her. "This next part's easy."

Enjoying the comfort of his closeness, Eve did relax. "This is nice," she said after a while, indicating the green shores on either side of the narrow waterway. "Restful."

"I've heard it called 'ditch crawling,'" Vic said. "You just sit back, steer, and enjoy the scenery."

"Nothing wrong with that. We've had enough excitement for one day."

On their starboard side, some people were picnicking. They waved. Here, too, were small boats, canoes and rowboats. Vic was very careful to proceed slowly so the Six Pack's wake wouldn't swamp them. They passed a camping area where they were hailed by two boys on bikes. The boys were following a path parallel to the canal. "Hey," one of them called. "Wanna race?"

Vic laughed and shook his head. "No thanks."

"Aw, come on. Just up to that big willow tree. Look, I'll even give ya a head start." He stopped his bike, waited thirty seconds, and yelled, "Here I come."

Seeing the boy gaining, Eve shook Vic's arm. "He's catching up, Vic. Go faster."

Vic's laughter filled the air. "I can't, not in this canal."

"But he's going to beat us."

Sure enough, the boy was now abreast and ready to pass. He chortled and waved derisively as he pulled ahead. He got to the tree a full ten seconds before they did.

"Damn," Eve said under her breath. Then she cupped her hands around her mouth and called to shore. "We let you win."

"Yeah, yeah . . ." the cyclist jeered.

"Rotten kid," she murmured under her breath, provoking another peal of laughter from Vic.

"I never pegged you as a cutthroat competitor," he said.

"I'm not. I was only kidding." That was mostly true, although the boy's dare had irked, and it would have been satisfying to beat him.

"It's not whether you win or lose . . ." Vic pronounced sonorously.

"I know, I know. It's how you play the game. Tell that to Maria," she said, and immediately wished she could retract the flip comment. "I mean because of her tennis," Eve added lamely.

"It's all right. I understand."

Did he? Then he must recognize what she was silently admitting to herself—that a double meaning could apply. Not tennis, but a different game in which Eve and Maria were rivals, and Vic was the prize. It was a hateful thought and she forced it out of her mind.

The weather suddenly changed. Skies turned gray and the wind picked up. It was late evening and beginning to rain when they were coming close to Whitehall. "If we hadn't lost all that time this morning," Vic said with a frown, "we would have made Ticonderoga by now. We'd better put up here for the night. I should be able to get in touch with Al at the Ticonderoga Marina . . . tell him we'll be there by noon tomorrow. Okay?"

As if he needed to ask. "Fine with me." It was foolish, but Eve felt as though she'd been given a reprieve.

On shore, Vic made the call. "No problem," he told Eve when he returned. "It's good I called. Al was worried about our being out in this weather. He'd booked us a couple of rooms at the marina up there, so he'll take one for the night. All's well."

"Good."

"I also checked on restaurants. With this weather, we'd better settle for the closest one." The rain had become a downpour. Vic's hair was dripping, his clothes drenched.

"First let's get you out of those wet things," Eve told him.

He gave her a sidelong glance and grinned. "What a great idea."

"That's *not* what I meant."

He caught her to him.

"It's still a great idea," he said against her lips.

They decided to eat in that evening.

The rain continued well into the night. The *Six Pack* lurched and groaned as her dock lines stretched with the wind, but Eve and Vic slept soundly, locked in each other's arms.

Morning came—with an end to Eve's reprieve.

The rain had stopped. The sky, cleared by last night's winds, was a bright blue canopy ornamented by a brilliant sun.

"Glorious, isn't it?" Vic said.

Feeling guilty that she'd hoped for more stormy weather, Eve agreed.

The morning's run was uneventful. Just beyond Whitehall, they went through the last lock on the Champlain Canal, then followed the channel through a fifteen-mile marshy stretch in the southern narrows of Lake Champlain. On either shore were the foothills of the Green and Adirondack mountains. Nothing happened to delay them, for which Eve should have been grateful, but wasn't.

Dr. Fraser must have been on the lookout for them. There he was on the dock waving his white baseball cap, indicating where they should pull in. He wore denim cutoffs and an oversized Columbia University sweatshirt. Eve remarked on how different he looked from the distinguished college professor whom she'd persuaded to let her lease the *Six Pack*.

"His sloppy sophomore look," Vic said. "That's what Al calls it. Says the *Six Pack* is his escape from convention."

Eve could easily sympathize with that sentiment. "There's no Mrs. Fraser, is there?" she asked.

"No."

"Was there ever?"

"No. Al's one of those old-fashioned bachelors."

Eve was about to say that was too bad, when Vic added, "He's a pretty happy guy."

Dr. Fraser certainly looked chipper at the moment. He helped secure the boat, then hopped aboard. "Well, now, how'd you two make out?"

Vic's glance at Eve signaled his awareness of the double meaning Al hadn't intended. With a straight face, he assured Al, "We made out fine."

"That problem you mentioned on the phone yesterday?" Al asked.

"Apparently just a quirk." Vic's description of what had occurred ended with a tribute to Eve's resourceful performance.

"Well, young lady . . ." Al said. "Sounds like you're losing your landlubber status. I guess Vic's a good teacher."

"Yes, he is." Among other things.

"The *Six Pack*'s not exactly built for luxury cruising." Al looked from one to the other with a teasing appraisal. "Hope you weren't too cramped, Eve."

"We managed all right, Dr. Fraser."

"Yes, I can see that." He gave her a bright smile. "But don't 'Dr. Fraser' me please, Eve. That's for the classroom. On the *Six Pack* with friends, it's 'Al.' Okay?"

"Sure."

"Al, what's your program?" Vic wanted to know.

"Just some leisurely gunkholing around the lake for a few days, maybe explore around Grand Isle. My sister lives in Burlington, so I'll pick her up day after tomorrow to spend the afternoon on the boat. Then I'll head down to meet you back here on Saturday, like we said."

"Sounds good."

"Want to come along? We could find shore accommodations at night."

Eve guessed that the invitation was offered out of politeness.

"Wouldn't think of it," Vic quickly replied. "We're going to take your car and drive up to Montreal, maybe stop at Shelburne. Eve loves playing tourist."

"Good," Al said. "I really appreciate you two taking this chunk of time to come up here." He turned to Vic.

"How did you manage to break away from work on such short notice?"

"By being the boss," Vic said with a grin. "Which reminds me. I'd better call and see what's happening back in the real world."

"Use the phone in my room. Come on. I'll show you."

"We should get our gear off," Vic said.

"Later. I'm not in a rush," said Al.

As they walked around to the motel units, Vic suggested that Al have the mechanic here take another look at the *Six Pack*'s engine, just to be doubly sure everything was all right. Al agreed.

Al's duffel bag was on the bed in the room, packed and ready. Eve excused herself to enjoy the luxury of washing up again in a real bathroom. She took her time. Vic was on the phone to his office when she came out. Something about his voice got her attention.

"What the hell are you talking about, Marty? . . . Was the call from Maria or from Mrs. Spezia? . . . So why didn't you say there were two calls? . . . Okay, okay . . ."

Vic's face was as grim as his voice. Eve felt a foreboding.

"Yeah, probably New Hampshire . . ." Vic was saying. "What number did she leave? Wait." He opened the night-table drawer and found a pad. "No pen," he said with frustration.

Al got one from his bag and handed it to him. Vic mouthed a thank-you.

"Once again with that number . . . Got it . . . and that crazy message, that was the second call, right? . . . Read it to me again . . ." He listened, his brow furrowed. "All right. Anything else? . . . Never mind the fax report from Atlanta." The person in Vic's office must have persisted. Impatiently, Vic said, "If you can't handle the insurance claim, it'll have to keep." Vic hung up.

"Problems at work?" Al asked.

"Nothing important."

Al's next question was the one Eve had in her mind also. "Personal? Something about Maria?"

That Al Fraser knew Maria wasn't a surprise. Didn't everyone know about Vic and Maria? Eve felt suddenly cold.

Frowning, Vic ran his fingers through his hair. "Just a phone call. She didn't leave a message."

"But you said . . ." Eve hesitated, "something about a crazy message."

"From Maria's mother." Vic shook his head slowly as if puzzling it out. "Marty said Mrs. Spezia called. She sounded very happy, but incoherent, and he had trouble understanding her. He asked if she wanted to leave a message. What Marty wrote down was, 'Tell Vittorio that Maria's test was good and the rabbit died.' "

"I gather that means Maria's pregnant," Al said dryly. "Though maybe not. They don't use rabbits anymore, do they?"

"Mrs. Spezia probably doesn't know that." Eve's voice sounded surprisingly contained to her ears. "She's an old-fashioned woman."

"She also said to be sure to tell *you*." Vic was speaking directly to Eve. "That you would want to know."

Eve nodded stiffly. The woman probably felt guilty about the conversation they'd had that night in Brooklyn, and the false hopes she had offered Eve.

"Maria never wanted kids," Vic said with angry confusion.

Had they discussed having children? Eve wondered. And in what context—a general conversation or specifically relating to their own situation? Eve's mind was in turmoil.

Vic picked up the phone and dialed the number he had written.

"I'll go get some things off the *Six Pack*," Eve said, and started for the door. This was a conversation she didn't want to hear.

"Eve . . ."

She ignored Vic's call. Outside, she started to run, stopping when she got to the boat and climbed aboard. But the *Six Pack* was no longer a sanctuary from the world. Panting, she leaned against the side, head bowed, as her breathing slowed. Gradually a numbing coldness crept through her body. The last few days had been like paradise, but it was a fool's paradise, and she had no one to blame but herself.

Eve had convinced herself that if Vic was uncertain how he felt about her, their being alone together would help to clarify his feelings. Eve knew she loved him and wanted to spend her life with him. Vic was the one who had choices to make, not Eve.

Oh, no, not me, she thought with self-directed sarcasm. She had made her choice all right. She had chosen a man who was involved with another woman. No. Correction—*she*, Eve, was the other woman, the intruder. God, how she hated that notion. She had never been in that position before.

Everyone had warned her about how Vic and Maria pulled apart but always got back together. Eve had happened to come along at the right time, the pulling-apart time. The wrong time for Eve. Now Maria was reining in. Maria didn't like to lose. She probably figured that after all this time, Vic belonged to her.

But no person can own another. Love isn't bondage. Vic had sworn that it was over between him and Maria. But he hadn't known about the baby then. Maria's ultimate weapon to keep Vic tied to her? No. Maria was not that kind of woman.

Eve gave a heavy sigh. There was no solace in putting Maria down as scheming and unscrupulous. It wasn't true. Maria's pregnancy might have been an accident, or perhaps something she subconsciously wanted. Vic had admitted that they'd slept together up until the time he'd met Eve.

Mrs. Spezia had sounded happy. Of course. She wanted her daughter to settle down. She was fond of Vic. What she'd had against him was that he hadn't been interested in marriage. Naturally she was assuming that would change.

Eve harbored the same assumption.

But weren't there alternatives? In today's world many women had babies and raised them as single parents. Maria and Vic might choose not to marry. Eve grasped at that idea; it meant that Vic wouldn't be lost to her.

She and Vic could continue with their plans for the next few days, discuss the matter thoroughly, then take the *Six Pack* back to New York, and Vic would work things out with Maria.

Sure! Sure, it could happen that way.

Eve hung on to that illusion for no more than ten seconds. She had been concentrating on herself, her own hurt and need and loss. There were two others, potentially three, who were primarily involved. If she loved Vic, why would she want to make it harder for him? He'd been obviously upset just now. His impatience gave him away, and his uncharacteristic disinterest in dealing with a business problem.

Eve could understand Vic feeling he was caught in a dilemma. He had convinced Eve that he cared for her, but they were really just beginning to know each other. A month ago, they'd been strangers. These last few days had been idyllic. They'd been so close, sharing humor and work and physical passion.

Days, not years. And measured against the long-standing relationship with Maria . . . ?

Eve remembered the gnawing little doubt she'd been repressing, how she had hoped something would delay their arrival here. The *Six Pack* was no longer their private island. They were back in the real world.

And her real world, she thought bitterly, awaited her back home in Leonardtown.

Their voices alerted her, giving her time to compose

herself before Vic and Al climbed on board. With no preamble, Vic told her, "Maria wasn't there. She might be back tonight, maybe not till tomorrow. I'll have to call again."

They stared at each other for a long moment. In his eyes, Eve read a worrisome brooding, but there was nothing she could do about it.

Then Vic said, "We're going to move the boat around to the mechanic's shed now."

"To get the engine checked out again," Al offered. He went over to the controls, and Vic started to undo the lines.

"Oh, let me get off first," Eve said. In answer to Vic's inquiring glance, she explained, "I think I'll go back to the room for a shower."

She darted into the cabin and gathered a few things, including her pocketbook, into a large straw bag. Al and Vic were talking in low voices. Snatches of the conversation came to her, but then Eve started to pay attention.

"I think you ought to stop speculating," Al was saying. "Go see Maria."

Impatiently, Vic asked, "How can I go to New Hampshire?"

"Simple. You have my car. Drive there."

"And what about Eve?"

She hated the note of frustration in Vic's voice.

There was a long pause. Eve barely made out Al's reply. "You've got a point there. It would be awkward to take her with you."

Awkward! Eve felt a coil tightening around her heart.

They'd moved out of earshot. Making some noise to alert them, Eve came out of the cabin. Vic was standing on the dock. He reached out to help Eve. Taking his hand, she held on tightly and stepped off, ending up close to him. She forced a tremulous smile. How she wanted him to say, "It'll be all right, Eve. I love you, and it'll be all right." But how could he? His expression told a different story.

"It won't take long to check out the engine," he said. "Are you all right?"

"Fine."

They both knew it was a lie.

THIRTEEN

By the time Eve reached the motel room, she had only one thought on her mind—to get away. For Vic's sake and her own. He had to come to grips with this new development without Eve's hovering presence distracting him. Let him go to New Hampshire if he wanted to, but there was no way she could go with him. Al was right about that. But she couldn't see herself sitting around here waiting for him to return, either. No, she had to go back to New York.

Eve quickly changed into the sandals, shirt, and pants she'd brought. Everything else would have to stay on the boat for now. Fortunately she'd had the presence of mind to take her handbag and wallet with her. As if she'd known all along what she had to do. With money, credit cards, and her driver's license, she should be able to find some way of getting back to New York. She would call for a taxi from the motel office and get to town to make arrangements.

Fortunately Vic was occupied with Al and the mechanic and she could avoid seeing him. What would be the point? Would he try to stop her? He might, and she would wonder, whatever protests he might offer, if he really wouldn't prefer having one less complication to deal with. Vic hated complications. No, it was better to dispense with good-byes. A short note would suffice.

All Eve could find to write on was a picture postcard advertising the marina motel. It was the kind one used for communications like, "Having a wonderful time." Ironic.

The space on the back allowed for only a few lines, but Eve's message was short.

Vic,
There's no point in my staying. You have enough on your mind without worrying about me. I'm going back to New York.

Eyes smarting, Eve paused, her pen suspended.
Sincerely . . . Love . . . ?
She caught her upper lip in her teeth, then simply signed her name.

In the office, the manager's wife heard Eve ask about calling a taxi and offered her a lift to town. Cheerful and garrulous, the woman kept chattering as she drove, apparently satisfied with her one-sided conversation and Eve's occasional murmured responses. Eve asked to be let off in the center of town.

"I'll be headin' back in about an hour if you want a lift," the woman said.

"I won't be going back," Eve's voice reflected the numbness in her heart.

"Aren't you off that little cruiser just came in? From New York City?"

"Yes."

The manager's wife was curious. "You're not going back on her?"

"No." The woman might mean well, but Eve had no desire to answer her questions.

"How're you getting home?"

That's what Eve was going to find out. "Depends on what's available. A car rental preferably. Is there a place in town?"

"Sure. There's a couple of 'em. Can't say as I blame you. Going through all those locks. Awful! My husband made me do it once. Never again. What a nightmare, right?"

Nightmare? No. These few days with Vic on the *Six Pack* were among the happiest Eve had ever known. The nightmare might be just starting.

But all Eve said was, "It wasn't so bad".

With a derisive snort, her companion said, "Yeah, sure. So why're you leaving?"

"I have some business to take care of back home." The business of getting on with her life—without Vic.

Near the bus station was a car rental agency where Eve leased a car that she could drop off in New York. The clerk gave her a map and directions. "Take 9N south to 87," he advised. "It's a real scenic route." Eve thanked him and left.

She noticed little of the scenic beauty as she drove. She thought longingly of the past few days, and despairingly of the future.

Vic read the note several times, letting the realization sink in. When Al came into the room, Vic was sitting on the bed, frowning at the postcard he still held.

"The guy in the office just told me that his wife gave Eve a lift into town," Al said. "What's up?"

"She's gone."

Al didn't understand. "To do some shopping maybe."

"No. Eve won't be coming back. She's gone," he repeated.

Al noticed the card Vic held. "Where?"

"Back to New York."

"Without you?"

Vic nodded. That was the idea. He stood up, tossed the card on the dresser, and made for the door.

"Where you going?" Al asked.

"To talk to the manager's wife."

Al went with him. They had to wait a half hour for the woman to return.

"Yeah," she told them. "I gave her a ride to town. Dropped her at a car rental place. She said she was going back to New York." The woman give Vic a suspicious look. "You didn't know she was going?"

He shook his head.

Suspicion deepened into disapproval. "I guess she thought you'd stop her."

As they left the office, Vic overheard the manager talking to his wife. "Boy," he said, "that lady sure must've hated cruising up here . . . even more than you."

"Don't be a jerk," his wife told him. "It's more than that. Jeez, what you guys make us go through."

A chance remark by a stranger, but it bothered Vic. What was he making Eve go through? She was in pain or she wouldn't have run off.

As they walked back to the boat, Al asked, "Would you have?"

"Would I have what?"

"Stopped Eve from leaving?"

"Damn right." Anger was infiltrating Vic's concern, then frustration because he didn't have the right to be angry.

"Vic, what's between you two? First, I figured a little summer fling. You know, fun and games. It's more than that?"

"Yes."

"And now Maria . . . ?"

"Yes, and now Maria." Frustration made him vehement. He balled his hands into fists. "Only exactly what the hell is going on, I don't know. And Eve could have waited until I found out. How did I get myself into this mess?"

"Through me, I'm afraid," the professor said ruefully. "I'm sorry I ever decided to rent out the *Six Pack* for the summer."

"So am I."

They had reached the boat. Al put his hand on Vic's arm. "Do you mean that?"

"Yes." Practically a groan. The part of him that had always avoided entanglements which could tie him down gave that answer.

But there was another part, a dimension that only Eve had ever fathomed, and under her touch, it had grown.

Vic shook his head in frustration and corrected himself. "No!"

He was *not* sorry that Eve had come to live on the *Six Pack*, that he'd gone from being impatient and amused to being intrigued, then captivated, and finally in love with her. She had evoked depths of passion and emotion he hadn't known he possessed. Without Eve, they would stagnate.

"So what's next?" Al asked. "New Hampshire?"

"I thought about it, but driving all that distance when Maria might not even be there doesn't make sense. For all I know, she could be heading back to New York. The guy on the phone wasn't sure where the hell she was." Vic had known Maria to change her mind on a moment's notice. "First, I want to talk to her on the phone." He looked at his watch. It was ten after two. But he had no idea when he could reach her at the number she'd left. The thought of waiting around for hours, perhaps overnight, was galling. "Hell, I'd go nuts sitting around here all day."

Al's look was questioning. Vic came to a decision. He didn't have to call Maria from here.

"I'm going back to New York," he said. That's where Eve was headed.

*   *   *

At the car-rental agency, the clerk said cheerfully, "Too bad you weren't around a couple of hours ago. A lady was here wanting to drive to New York, same as you. Maybe you could've hooked up together and saved on driving and gas." Vic's frown caused him to add hastily, "Just a thought. Sometimes it's better to be on your own." He glanced down at Vic's credit card. "Right, Mr. Adesso?"

Vic gave a curt nod.

Al Fraser walked him to where the rental car was parked. "Sorry about lousing up your plans," Vic told him.

"Don't sweat it. Besides, you didn't louse up anything. I'm still going to take the boat out."

"Don't forget," Vic said, "your dockage bill here is on my charge."

Al had told Vic not to worry about getting the *Six Pack* back to New York. It could stay at the marina in Ticonderoga until the end of summer session.

"We'll work it out," said Al. "It's Eve whose summer plans are spoiled. With the *Six Pack* up here, she's got no place to stay."

"My apartment or the *Hippolyta*. She can have her pick." But Vic wasn't at all sure she would accept either one.

"I'll be in touch," he told Al. They said good-bye and Vic was on his way.

Vic had been speeding on the interstate. Fortunately, the traffic cop had let him off with a warning. After that, he set the cruise control at sixty-five and stayed there. There was no way he was going to catch up to Eve, so what was the point? At seven o'clock, he stopped to call New Hampshire, but Maria was still out. He picked up a hamburger to eat in the car but ended up throwing most of it out at the next rest stop.

Vic tried to channel his thoughts. In his business, he prided himself on thinking through all aspects of a situation. He needed to do that here. If Maria was pregnant with his child . . . That was the message, but he hadn't yet accepted the reality.

Of course, it was possible. Unplanned pregnancies happened. The last time they'd been together was several months ago, but Maria might not have guessed she was pregnant earlier. She had once mentioned how her strenuous workouts sometimes made her skip periods.

Her strange behavior recently, was this what was behind it? Perhaps unconsciously, the changes in her body had been affecting Maria's thought processes, making her question her way of life, preparing her for the need to alter it.

The irony was that Vic, too, had been thinking of alteration, but along different lines—like acknowledging that what he and Maria had was affection, not love. They need not be lovers; they could be friends. They should have reached an understanding months ago, before he'd met Eve. But it had not happened. They had let things drift.

Back then, Maria would probably have agreed with Vic's assessment of their relationship.

But now . . .

Vic wondered about Maria's state of mind. Did she feel caught, resentful? Marty had said Mrs. Spezia had been overjoyed. Was Maria overjoyed, too? Vic had never subscribed to the idea that pregnancy was the woman's problem. Of course, he'd never pictured himself in this kind of predicament, but if Maria wanted this baby, Vic would support her decision.

Then what?

His head was spinning. The car veered, bumping onto the warning lane dividers, and Vic forced himself to concentrate on driving. It was late and he was tired. He was incapable of thinking too far ahead. It would be after ten by the time he got to the city. Best to concentrate on two things, talking to Maria and finding Eve.

Vic tried to fathom Eve's motive in leaving. He guessed she had removed herself so he could be free to determine what he had to do. The gesture magnified his guilt for hurting her.

On the other hand, perhaps all she wanted was to get away from him. Did she feel betrayed? But even so, Eve shouldn't have left like that, without giving him a chance to talk to her.

Vic wasn't sure what he wanted to say to Eve right now. Except for one thing. Whatever else was to happen it was important that she know he loved her and that these last few days had been real and wonderful.

And Eve's thoughts on this long drive back? Primarily regrets? He hoped not. Perhaps she'd reconsidered and wanted to see him. Vic clutched at the hope that he would find her at the marina, waiting for him.

It was still daylight when Eve got to the marina. She had made good time driving down. Returning the rental car at LaGuardia Airport in Queens had taken an extra half hour, but she'd gotten a cab immediately, and traffic into Manhattan was exceptionally light.

Eve had called Greta from the rental office. For once her friend didn't bombard her with questions. When Eve told her where she was and asked to stay overnight, Greta said to come ahead. The questions, Eve knew, would come later. "I'll be an hour or so," she told Greta. "I've got to pick up my car."

The taxi dropped Eve in front of the marina office. Her car was in the parking area. Eve glanced down the dock to the *Six Pack*'s empty berth. Suddenly she remembered the suitcase Vic had stored on his sailboat. And her stone. She still had his key, so there was no reason to leave her things.

Eve had to make two trips. As she walked down the

dock, her mind slipped back, remembering her impressions and feelings when she'd first arrived at the marina, that mixture of apprehension and anticipation at the start of a new adventure. It seemed so long ago. Her adventure had taken an unexpected turn.

Eve had hoped to get away without encountering anyone. She'd just put her things in the trunk when she heard a familiar "Yoo hoo", and saw Loretta bearing down on her. That settled the question of how to return Vic's key, but she would try to break away quickly.

Almost out of breath with her hurrying effort, Loretta asked, "How come you're back? Where's Vic? You didn't have an accident with the *Six Pack*, did you?"

"No accident."

"You're all right?"

How to answer that? Eve shrugged. "Yeah, sure."

Loretta wasn't deceived. "No, you're not. What happened?"

"It's a long story."

"I got plenty of time."

Loretta's round face was creased with concern. Eve couldn't just brush her off.

"Come on," Loretta said. "I'll make you a cup of coffee."

Eve let herself be led to the *Someday* where Loretta got the percolator going.

"You know, Eve, it's lucky I saw you. We'd probably have called the cops, Bo or me." At Eve's shocked reaction, Loretta explained. "Your car. If we'd seen it missing, we'd've thought it was stolen."

An understandable assumption, Eve realized. "I'm sorry. I didn't think. Wouldn't that have been something— getting arrested for stealing my own car?" It was a weak attempt at humor. Suddenly the exhaustion that had been building up all day hit Eve and she felt completely drained.

Loretta held back while Eve savored the hot coffee. She

poured a second cup, then gently prodded. "So tell me. How long did it take to get up there?"

"Four days."

"Good trip?"

"Yes." Eve's mind flashed back to the happy interlude, the talking and laughter, the sharing. And at night . . . falling asleep in Vic's arms. "Yes," she repeated softly. "A wonderful trip."

"And?"

Eve took in a deep breath and exhaled on a sigh. "And then it was over," she said with despairing matter-of-factness.

"You were supposed to stay and come back together."

"Things don't always turn out as they're supposed to."

"You left Vic up there?"

Eve nodded. "He might be going to New Hampshire."

"What for?"

"Maria's there."

Loretta's expression showed surprise, exasperation, and concern. "If you don't beat all. The three of you . . . Vic and Maria, too. Now, why'd you let him go, Eve?"

"I've got no claim on Vic."

"Bullshit. Excuse the expression. Of course, you have a claim. You love him. You don't have to give way to Maria."

"Nor she to me. Loretta, they've been together for years."

"There's all kinds of being together. If Maria and Vic had wanted to make it permanent, they'd have done it long ago."

Eve shook her head; she'd heard this before. "It's different now."

"What's different?"

Eve blurted it out. "Maria's pregnant."

Loretta's mouth dropped. "Holy moly!" Surprise gave way to sympathy. "Eve, I'm sorry."

"Me, too," Eve said ruefully. She would have to practice pretending she didn't care. At the moment, she couldn't fake it.

"What's Vic going to do?" asked Loretta.

"I don't know. That's for him and Maria to decide."

"What are *you* going to do?"

"I'm going home to Leonardtown—where I belong."

"Tonight? When you've been driving all day?"

Loretta's disapproval was mollified when Eve explained that she would stay overnight with friends in the city. She didn't mention them by name. "I'll head home in the morning," she said.

As expected, Greta pressed Eve for details soon after she arrived at the Avedons. George had diplomatically disappeared so the two women could talk. Briefly Eve explained why she had left.

Expecting a strident, "I told you so", Eve was relieved at Greta's more restrained reaction.

Greta shook her head sadly and said, "You don't need this grief; you never should have gone up there."

"Maybe not." But inwardly Eve knew she didn't mean it. Whatever happened, she could not regret having had those days on the *Six Pack* with Vic. The news about Maria would have reached them wherever they were.

"You love him, don't you?" Greta asked.

"Yes."

"What are you going to do?"

That question again. As if she had a choice. "I'm going home."

"What about the things you left on the boat?"

"Loretta will collect whatever's there and send them on to me when the *Six Pack* gets back."

"When is that?"

"I don't really know."

Would Vic go to New Hampshire and then back to Ticonderoga? Perhaps Maria would make the trip down-

river with him. But Maria didn't like that kind of cruising.
So maybe . . .

Eve stopped herself. All those torturous *maybe's*. What
was the point?

Vic hated feeling helpless. Eve wasn't at the marina.
He still hadn't talked to Maria. He was tired and irritable.
He'd rushed back to New York, and all he could do was
sit here and wait. The sound of footsteps on the dock got
him to race outside, but it was only Loretta.

"I brought you a sandwich," she said as she came
aboard. She followed him into the lounge, put the sandwich on a dish, and placed it in front of him. Vic took
one bite, then forgot about eating.

"Are you sure Eve didn't mention her friend's name?"
he asked.

Loretta shook her head. "For the umpteenth time, no.
She never said."

With a guttural sound of frustration, Vic smacked the
table with the heel of his hand. It was probably that couple
he'd met in the marina office the other day, the ones whom
Rader had introduced as "Eve's dear friends." Glen must
have mentioned their names. Dammit. Why couldn't he
remember? Because he'd been so damned agitated, that's
why—angry at seeing Eve with Rader and at Rader's proprietary manner with her.

He hadn't been able to get in touch with Glen, either.
He'd tried, but gotten Glen's answering machine. "Strike
three," he muttered.

"What'd you say?" asked Loretta.

"Nothing." Then, angrily, "You shouldn't have let
Eve leave here."

"Hey, simmer down, friend. Don't take your problems
out on me. Eve can do what she wants, and if she doesn't
want any part of you right now, that's her privilege. What
the heck did you expect, anyway?"

Loretta left before he could apologize.

Vic plowed his fingers through his tangled hair. He had no answer to Loretta's parting question. After all, he had no right to expect anything from Eve.

Greta was reluctant to let Eve leave in the morning. "Stay till Saturday," she coaxed as they sat at the breakfast table. "You still look beat."

Considering her sleepless hours tossing around on the living-room sofa, Eve wasn't surprised.

"Thanks, but I'd rather get going."

"What about your tuition at the New School?" George asked. "Shouldn't you get a refund?"

Ever practical George. But he was right. Today was the first session of her class. Eve decided on a detour to the school to inquire about getting at least some of her fee refunded.

Fortunately, both Greta and George had to go to work so they didn't dally over good-byes.

Things were looking up, Eve told herself when she found a parking space a block from the school. Determined to stop dwelling on the past, Eve was making a conscious effort to think positively. Hadn't she read once that smiling and laughing, even with forced cheerfulness, was therapeutic? She looked about her. It was a bright, cloudless morning, without the usual summer mugginess. The streets were crowded, people heading for work, students rushing to class. The kind of energy she had always loved about the city. Eve had expected to be part of it this summer, but . . .

She let the thought trail away.

Inside the school's front lobby, someone called, "Hey, Eve. Wait up."

Resplendent in a jungle print jumpsuit with floppy trousers, Reva hurried over.

"Hi. You're not late so don't rush," Reva said. "There's a notice on the door. No class."

"It's been canceled?"

"Yeah. And for two more sessions after this. Smirnoff had an accident. He's in the hospital." Jack Smirnoff was the instructor for their sculpting class. "D'you think he's related to the vodka Smirnoffs?" Reva didn't expect an answer. "Anyway, they're getting a replacement, Lil Johnson, but she can't take over till July so they're re-scheduling the class."

"Really?" Eve frowned. "Then maybe I can get a total refund," she speculated.

"Hey, don't do that. This Johnson's supposed to be terrific—better than Smirnoff."

"Maybe so, but I can't stay." Eve explained that she was on her way back to Maryland, and had stopped at the school to withdraw from the class.

"Why?"

"I lost my summer rental." That was all Reva had to know.

"That boat you told me about? It sounded so cool. What happened?"

"It just didn't work out."

"That's too bad," Reva commiserated. Then, in re-sponse to a sudden idea, her mouth curved into a broad smile. "I got a brainstorm," she announced. "I get them periodically, like menstrual cramps. You can stay with me."

"What?"

"You can move into my place. Not till the brat vacates, but that's twelve days from now. The brat's my daughter, Didi. She's off on one of those youth cycling trips through Europe. Imagine burning your butt on a bicycle seat for three weeks. And after that she's spending a month with a French family in Marseilles, if they can stand her for that long. Anyway, she's leaving so her room'll be free. My place is on Tenth, real convenient." Reva completed her enthusiastic recitation with an affirmative nod, then added, "So you can go home for a couple of weeks and come back *chez moi. Mi casa es su casa.* How's that for a trilingual invitation?''

Eve had to smile. "Great. But I really couldn't."

"Why not? Hey, I'd be glad of the company. Didi can be one huge pain, but . . ." she gave a helpless shrug, "I miss her when she's not around. The house is too damn quiet. Know what I mean?"

Thinking of the empty house awaiting her in Leonardtown, Eve nodded.

"It's a deal then?" Reva asked.

"Reva, we hardly know each other."

"So what?" Reva must have guessed that Eve's resistance was fading. "We'll get along. Trust me, Eve. I'm a good judge of character. What're you smiling at?"

"I thought New Yorkers were supposed to be suspicious and unfriendly."

"They are," said Reva with a huge grin. "I'm the wonderful exception. What do you say?"

"Yes." Eve surprised herself, then hedged, "I think."

"What's to think about? We'll have a ball." She took Eve's arm. "Come on. We'll take a walk over and you can inspect the premises."

Reva would not be denied.

"What's your daughter going to say?" Eve asked when they got to the apartment.

"Hey, I'm the one pays the rent," was Reva's answer.

But Didi, a dynamic younger version of her mother, applauded the idea. "Great," she said. "Mom can use the company. She gets lonely when I'm not around." Didi planted a kiss on her mother's cheek, waved to Eve, and rushed off to meet a friend.

The apartment was spacious, with comfortable furniture and cheerful colors. Reva showed Eve her daughter's room. It had purple walls, a black ceiling, and track lighting. "The decor is what I call Neon Psychedelic," Reva said. "Think you can stand it? Didi says it gives her good vibes."

Eve smiled. She could use some good vibes.

An hour later, Eve said good-bye. She got in her car and headed downtown for the Holland Tunnel. Rush hour was over, and the traffic was moving. Soon she'd be leaving the city behind—its vitality and excitement, the variety of people, from derelicts to millionaires. But not for long. Eve would have her summer in New York after all. Instead of moping around her small town, she would come back.

She couldn't let herself give in to despair. Vic had been part of her life for such a short time. Surely she'd get over him. Eve had already come through an irrevocable loss of a loved one. She was a survivor, wasn't she?

But this time was different; Vic was lost only to *her*. Others would see him, hear his voice, enjoy his attention. She had to accept that.

Vic would go on with his life, and she had to get on with hers.

FOURTEEN

There were no provisions in the house, so Eve stopped in town to buy a few basic groceries before going home. Across from the market was her cousin's storefront office, "David Bittner, Attorney-at-Law".

Funny, how Dave and Vic had known each other in college. Eve decided to drop in and let her cousin know she was home.

Dave gave her his usual bear-hug greeting. "I thought you weren't coming back till late August."

"Well, I . . ."

"Aha! Big city got to be too much for you?"

"Not at all." As usual, his teasing riled her. "My class is rescheduled. I'll be going back in two weeks." She changed the subject. "How's Janet?"

"Fine."

"Maybe I'll stop and say hello on my way home."

Eve and David's wife were good friends.

"Then you'll have to detour down to St. Mary's," Dave said.

"Oh, right. I forgot."

Janet Bittner was one of the directors of the St. Mary's City Pageant. Every year during the tourist season, the historic town re-created its past as the first capital of the colony under Lord Baltimore. Visitors could wander around the riverfront and visit the tavern and inn, the courthouse, and a replica of the ship that carried the early settlers over from England. Janet, who taught at St. Mary's College, spent her summers helping with the festival.

"As usual, I'm the forgotten husband until it's over," Dave said mournfully, adding that his wife would be staying over in St. Mary's through the weekend.

"Then I guess I can't wangle myself an invitation to dinner."

"You just did," Dave proclaimed happily. "Maryland crab cakes at The Shack. You and me, my treat. How about it?"

Eve accepted at once. It had nothing to do with the fact that Dave and Vic had once been friends. She was fond of her cousin, and she didn't want to be alone tonight.

Eve's house was an old-fashioned Victorian with curlicue trim and a spacious front porch, the kind of house that tourists called quaint and stopped their cars in front of to take pictures. It was a pretty cottage with an air of stability and permanence.

Earthbound, Eve thought as she pulled into her driveway. But, of course, it was, she chided herself. Houses were supposed to be. This was her home, her haven. But inside the house, she felt strangely jumpy. After putting away the groceries, Eve went around opening all the windows. But the air that came in was heavy and oppressive.

She went upstairs, then back down, wandering from room to room. The house seemed vast and empty. She thought of the small cabin on the *Six Pack* and the man who filled it with his presence. He'd filled her life as well. His absence left a void.

Temporarily, Eve told herself. Not that any other man could take Vic's place, but there were other places in her life, and other people. She had her work, friends, activities she enjoyed. This hollowness in her heart would eventually disappear.

Eve ate ravenously. Dave laughed at her appetite and ordered her another crab cake. She'd eaten very little since leaving Ticonderoga. *Hunger pangs, not heartbreak, that's what's wrong with you,* she told herself facetiously, wishing it were true. That kind of hunger was easily satisfied.

With conscious forbearance, Eve had kept herself from mentioning Vic all through dinner. She let Dave dominate the conversation with his detailed description of a particularly involved case he was working on. But when coffee and dessert came, Dave switched topics. "Enough law talk. Tell me about life in the big city. What's it like living on a boat?"

"Interesting."

"That's all? One word? I bet you met all kinds of characters."

"I did."

Dave waited expectantly.

The words tumbled out. "As a matter of fact, one of them is someone you used to know."

"Yeah? Who's that?"

"Victor Adesso."

No more forbearance. It was as though Eve needed to say his name, needed to talk about him.

"Adesso? You're kidding?"

"No. He has a sailboat in the marina where I stayed."

Dave asked for details. Eve made everything sound very casual. If Dave suspected anything, he didn't let on.

"How about that?" Dave marveled. "Last time I saw Vic was four years ago in New York, right before Janet and I got married. He was with this classy blonde . . ."

"Maria Spezia."

"Right. You met her, too?"

"Yes."

"So they're still on, are they?"

"So it would appear." The forced smile strained Eve's face.

Happily, Dave started reminiscing about college and some of his and Vic's escapades. Eve listened avidly, trying to picture Vic at twenty as Dave described him—daring, fiercely independent, ready for a fight or a good time.

"Come on over to the house," Dave said after paying the check. "I'll dig out my album of college pictures. Vic's in a lot of them."

"I'd better pass," Eve told him. "I'm really beat."

She had to stop letting Vic dominate her thoughts. Looking at photographs wouldn't help.

Dave dropped her in front of her house. "What're you going to do with yourself for the next couple of weeks?" he asked.

Her mind drew a blank. "I don't know."

Later that night, a call from Dave's wife provided a partial answer.

"My prayers have been answered," Janet said, and proceeded to describe the pageant's dilemma of being short several key performers.

"Wonderful," Janet said with relief. "I couldn't believe it when Dave told me you'd come home just when we really need you. You know all the parts so you can fill in anyplace. Eve, you're a godsend."

"A two-week godsend," Eve told her. "Don't forget I'm going back to New York."

"Whatever. By then maybe we'll have a full roster again. In the meantime, we've got you. Can you come tomorrow?"

"Sure. What time?"

"Early. We'll have breakfast. I'm at the guest house. Eve, thanks. You're wonderful."

It was nice to hear.

Eve hung up and got ready for bed. The festival would give her something to do while she was here. She needed to keep busy.

It had been a good idea to start out before sunup, Vic thought. The Jersey Turnpike traffic was still sparse. He'd be in the Washington area before noon, and from there it was less than two hours to Leonardtown. He had to see Eve. Calling on the phone wouldn't do. What he had to say needed to be said in person.

Eve left the house early in the morning. She was glad she had agreed to help Janet out. Having a purposeful activity on which to focus was better than moping around. She'd stopped first at the Visitor's Center to say hello. She knew practically everyone associated with the St. Mary's summer pageant. Her next stop was at the tobacco plantation, where Jim Fenton greeted her warmly. He was already in costume, as were the others who portrayed the Spray family. An industrial arts teacher during the school year, Jim spent his summers playing the role of planter, Godiah Spray. He gave Eve a warm greeting.

"Janet said she'd drafted you into service. Great. It'll be like old times."

During college and for a couple of years afterward, Eve had taken part in the summer festival. She knew every female character part from the gracious and elegant Lady Baltimore to a sniveling indentured servant. She'd even taken over a masculine role when needed. It had been fun.

"Yes," she said. "Like old times."

The words lingered in Eve's mind after she said goodbye and headed for the guest house where Janet was waiting.

Like old times?

Back then, assuming another identity had been a lark to Eve. She'd loved the playacting. The participants were trained to stay in character at all times, not just during their dramatic skits. They would roam the festival grounds and engage visitors in conversation, but always with the accent and style of the seventeenth-century settlers they portrayed. Sometimes the younger players would keep up the masquerade when they were off duty and out of costume—just for fun.

A lifetime ago, Eve thought regretfully. But maybe she could revive some of that youthful spirit. If nothing else, it would be a relief to shed Eve Marsdon and be someone else for a little while.

"You're here," Janet cried when Eve walked into the cheerful dining hall. "I was starting to panic."

Eve looked at her watch. "I'm only five minutes late."

"So I panic easily."

Janet Bittner was the opposite of her large, good-natured husband. Small, dark, and determined, she was a take-charge person. Completely self-involved, Janet showed little interest in why Eve had come home. It was enough that she was here when Janet needed her.

After a breakfast of freshly baked danish and coffee, Eve said, "Okay, I'm ready. What have you got for me?"

"Since you've done them all, I figured you wouldn't care what part you played."

"Well, I wouldn't mind getting into some Lady Baltimore finery."

"That wig and heavy costume in this heat! I wouldn't do that to you," said Janet with suspicious righteousness.

"Oh? What then?"

"Maggie Tolliver."

Eve frowned, sighed, then gave a fatalistic shrug. "It figures."

"Do you mind?" Janet asked.

"Given a choice . . ."

"That was a rhetorical question," Janet hastily interrupted. "We've already shifted people around, and I'm counting on you for Maggie. Besides, it's a much meatier part." Coaxingly, she added, "Everyone always said you were the best Maggie Tolliver ever."

"Sure, sure," said Eve. "I'm a natural for the part."

"Come on then. Your costume's in my room. You can change there. Need my help?"

"No. Go on about your business."

"Okay. We've got six tour buses coming, and there's a couple of scout groups scheduled. Plus the usual tourist carloads."

Programmed events usually started at noon, but the practice was to have the costumed players engaging in typical activities around the grounds and in the reconstructed buildings. The flavor of past life was conveyed in casual encounters and conversations with visitors.

Janet held out a printed page. "Here's the listing of today's events."

Eve glanced at the program. No surprises. Her own shining hour would come at two-thirty when the captain of the sailing vessel, the *Maryland Dove*, would offer his human cargo, namely, indentured servant Maggie Tolliver, for sale to the highest bidder. But Maggie would be wandering about the area all day, complaining about her plight to anyone who would listen, hoping to find a sympathetic master to bid for her.

"When you're ready, stroll down to Farthing's Ordinary," Janet told her, using the seventeenth-century name for the inn that provided "dyett and drink" to travelers in the past, and refreshments for today's tourists.

"Okay."

"How long will you be?"

With a shrug and a smile, Eve replied, "Just long enough to transform myself into a sniveling servant girl."

Well, you wanted a change, Eve told herself caustically, as she got herself into Maggie Tolliver's darned and ragged brown skirt. The clumsy buckled shoes were too big and the shirred white blouse too tight. Over the blouse went a scruffy velvet vest with crossed ties under the bosom. Maggie's outfit didn't fit Eve very well, but the bereft attitude of the lowly servant, she thought ironically, might be considered a match. Except that she was determined not to let Eve Mardson remain bereft.

She finished dressing and looked at herself in the mirror. Hair too neat, she decided, and used her fingers to twist the neatness into an untidy mess. There, that was better. She tried out her Maggie look, shoulders sagging and mouth arched down in a perpetual whine. Good. She had it down pat. She allowed herself a smile of satisfaction. In a kind of reverse psychology, assuming Maggie's downtrodden personality made Eve feel better, being a contrast to the strength of her own character.

Eve left the guest house and headed for the Governor's Field exhibit area. The day was overcast and windy, threatening rain. She took a meandering path that followed the St. Mary's River. A small sailboat was putting out from the opposite shore. The mainsail and jib caught the wind and billowed out. She paused to watch. So graceful. Would she ever be able to see a sailboat slicing through the water without thinking of that morning sail with Vic? Or hear the whirring sound of a power boat without its conjuring up vivid memories of the two of them cruising on the *Six Pack*?

Her vision blurred from a hot film of tears. Eve told herself that as these memories faded, so would the hurt and this agonizing sense of loss. She couldn't suddenly tear Vic out of her heart, but she had to accept the fact that he was no longer part of her life.

Eve continued on her way. As she approached the replica of the State House of 1676 and the main exhibit area, she saw other costumed players up and about. Eve waved or stopped to greet those she knew. In front of the dock was the outdoor theater area where the Maryland Shakespeare Festival put on its summer performances. And at the dock was the *Maryland Dove*, a replica of the square-rigged sailing ship that had brought English settlers to St. Mary's City in 1634. She recognized Mike Clemens in the costume of Captain Richard Rowe. Mike taught in the college's sailing school.

He was talking to a group of a dozen tourists, describing the rigors of the journey from England and how seasick his passengers had been. "But they're a hardy lot and bore up well." Suddenly, he spied Eve. "Except for that one," he yelled. "That puking, miserable creature ne'er stopped her wailing except to eat and sleep."

"Eeyuuuu," Eve whined, immediately falling into her role. She went closer and appealed to the crowd. "As if I could keep any victuals in my poor stomach, nor close my eyes without being toppled about from all that heavin' and lurchin'. The storms were like to pull apart the ship's timbers and send us all to the bottom of the sea."

The captain gave a disdainful shake of his head. "Nonsense. This vessel is as staunch and seaworthy as can be found in the colonies. Which is more than I can say for you, my girl."

"Eeyuuu," Maggie wailed. "I'm a good girl, I am."

The audience enjoyed the continuing exchange. In playing Maggie for laughs, Eve was following the traditional practice of portraying her as a caricature, sniveling, unattractive, and pathetic.

"Two-thirty in the afternoon. Mind you not be tardy," the captain told her sternly as she turned to leave. "And wash your face and comb your hair before you come." To his listeners, he explained, "That's the time of the sale, here on the *Dove*. You will all be welcome. The wench's passage fee was to be paid for by Amos Jarvis who had contracted for her services, but the old fellow died of the pleurisy last month. Mayhap someone will offer enough for this sorry creature to pay my expenses in bringing her over. What d'you say, sir?" he asked, prodding a portly man in plaid shorts and a loud shirt.

"Can you not use a servant girl to help with the butter-churning and boiling of the wash?"

The tourist guffawed and said his wife bought her butter in the supermarket and has a washing machine for clothes.

"Truly?" the captain said with pretended astonishment. "They have such things in your colony? What manner of mechanism can do such work?"

Eve smiled to herself as she walked off. Mike would stay in character no matter how the conversation went. Ad-Libbing like this was part of the fun.

Eve entered the tavern room of Farthing's Ordinary where a robust Mrs. Farthing was holding forth. "It's a hard life, with the cooking and the cleaning and the washing. A hundred times I've told Mr. Farthing that he must buy us a female servant, but we had not the goods to trade or money to spare before. Now that we do," she said with a nod in Eve's direction, "there's naught worth bidding for."

Eve's cue. "I'm a good girl, I am, Mistress Farthing."

"A sturdy wench is what I need."

Eve flexed her arms. "I'm stronger than I look."

"You'll need to be if you go to Godiah Spray's plantation."

"Oh, please. Mrs. Farthing. I don't want to work in the fields. There's worms and snakes outside."

"And plenty of two-legged worms and snakes inside as well," said Mrs. Farthing with a snort. "Liars and thieves and traffickers with Satan. There's one such on trial in the County Court this afternoon, girl. Best ye be there and see what happens to wrongdoers."

With a frightened expression, Eve curtsied and said, "Yes, mum."

The arrival of Lord and Lady Baltimore, resplendent in ornately decorated costumes, diverted the attention of the tourists, and Eve slipped away.

The morning passed quickly. At noontime, Farthing's Arbor was crowded, every table filled with visitors partaking of the seventeenth-century chowders and "potages", or twentieth-century sandwiches. The rain had held off, but the clouds still looked ominous. The raw weather didn't dampen the spirits of the Brownie troop picnicking near the river. Two colonial youths had just finished a jousting game and were talking to the children. Just as Eve joined them, the young men were enticed away by a couple of pert colonial wenches.

Mrs. Elderberry, the troop leader, introduced the indentured servant, Maggie Tolliver.

"What's a 'denture servant'?" asked one of the children.

Eve explained about the contract that bound her to service for seven years and the captain's seeking to sell that contract to the highest bidder.

A spritely little girl shook her head with disapproval. "What if you don't like who takes you?"

"There's naught I can do. My fate is not in my hands."

That answer didn't satisfy the child. "That's awful."

"Of course, Maggie may not have to serve all seven years, Jennifer," Mrs. Elderberry said brightly. "Now, if some young colonist were in need of a wife and fancied Maggie, he could buy out her contract and marry her."

Giving Maggie a critical once-over, Jennifer said, "If you want to get someone to marry, maybe you'd better put on some red lipstick and fix your hair nicer."

Very seriously, Eve said, "Sage advice, for which I thank you."

"And buy a prettier dress."

"But there are no shops in town and Maggie has no money," Mrs. Elderberry said. "Remember, girls, she lives in different circumstances than you all do."

"But she *has* to do something," Jennifer insisted. To Maggie, she said, "Don't let them push you around."

"There's naught I can do," Eve said again.

"Pfhhh," said Jennifer with a disgusted look.

Mrs. Elderberry urged the children to finish their lunch

so they could get seats at the state house for the county trial. As Eve prepared to leave, the troop leader apologized for her outspoken charge. "Jennifer obviously doesn't understand the strictures of colonial life."

What really riled Jennifer, Eve suspected, was Maggie's abject acceptance and unwillingness to do anything to help herself. Why, Eve wondered, did Maggie have to be portrayed as such a sad sack, pathetically surrendering to the will of others? Couldn't she try to manipulate the strictures that bound her, find ways to exercise at least some control over her destiny?

Eve realized she was becoming impatient with Maggie Tolliver. "Put on some lipstick," Jennifer had advised. Eve smiled at the anachronism. But why shouldn't Maggie try to make herself more attractive? According to the script the players went by, Maggie would go to the Farthings, since Godiah Spray refused to bid more than a paltry sum. And poor sniveling Maggie was supposed to look forward gratefully to her future as a scullery maid.

Well, not this time!

FIFTEEN

Eve was deliberately a few minutes late getting down to the *Dove* where a crowd had assembled to witness the sale of the indentured servant. Mrs. Elderberry's Brownie troop was among them. Captain Rowe was keeping the visitors entertained with stories about the *Dove*'s first voyage from England with her sister ship, the *Ark*. He interrupted himself when he caught sight of Maggie.

"Here she is," he cried and then did a double take. Eve had abandoned her Maggie Tolliver droop. Shoulders back, she assumed a swinging stride with as much jauntiness as Maggie's too-large shoes allowed. Even in the same scruffy clothes, there was a different look to Maggie—hair combed, cheeks pinched and ruddy, lips smiling boldly.

"Make haste and stop your strutting, Maggie," the captain ordered. "You're late, girl. There were those as feared you'd run away."

"Nay," she replied. "I'd not cheat those good folk from their show." Stepping smartly onto the deck, she added, "Nor myself from seeking a good master."

The captain gave her a closer appraisal. This was not the Maggie he'd expected, but he quickly picked up on the change. ''Well, now,'' he exclaimed, ''the girl has got a bit of spirit after all. Seems she's shed her meekness along with her greenish pallor.''

With a toss of black curls, Eve said, ''I'm a good girl, I am,'' but this time Maggie's familiar refrain was a boast, not a whine. ''Just trying to do the best for meself is all.''

Jennifer, standing close by, grinned and gave Eve a thumbs-up gesture.

What followed was a departure from the usual scenario of a short, humorous bidding contest between Godiah Spray and the innkeeper Farthing, with Captain Rowe urging them on. Maggie started speaking up for herself.

''I'm a good worker, I am. I can clean a house, cook a stew, churn, sew, and tend to young'uns.''

''All well and good, my lass.'' It was Mistress Spray with a critical scowl. ''But what we're needin' at the plantation is a healthy worker to keep the vegetable garden and help in the fields.'' To the captain, she said, ''This one doesn't look fit enough for hard work.''

''That's naught but vestiges of the seasickness,'' Captain Rowe assured the planter's wife. ''The minute Maggie's feet touched dry land, she perked up. Why just this morning, the girl had a greenish cast, and see how she's recovered.'' He put his arm around Maggie, who did a pert pirouette and disengaged herself. ''There's a comely lass here,'' he said with an appreciative leer.

''How you talk, sir,'' Maggie said. Her smile coaxing, she turned to the innkeeper, Farthing. ''The tavern, sir, would suit me better than the plantation, and I'd give good service, I would.'' The innkeeper smiled back, but his wife frowned.

''Don't overstep your place, Maggie,'' the captain warned in a loud whisper. ''What suits you is of no consequence.''

''It is to me,'' was Maggie's fierce reply.

Spray started the bidding with one silver shilling. Captain Rowe gave a derogatory snort. "One shilling for such a comely lass?"

"There's no use for comeliness in a tobacco field," said Mistress Spray tartly.

The innkeeper countered with a higher offer, and a brief competition ensued. Captain Rowe encouraged Farthing's bidding. "Having a saucy serving wench would surely induce your patrons to linger over their victuals and ale. And she's like to bring the unwed farmers in for a bit of relaxation."

"Don't be putting notions in the girl's head," Mistress Farthing objected stoutly. "You'll have her looking for a husband to buy out her contract beforetimes."

"At a profit to you were he to double what you give for her," the captain cagily pointed out.

"Two silver shillings," Farthing offered.

"And you, Master Spray?" asked the captain.

Ignoring his wife's restraining hand, the planter added a bale of tobacco to his last offer. Farthing countered with a higher bid of half a crown. The innkeeper was supposed to win, leading to the next part of the program where Mistress Farthing, for the benefit of the visitors, takes the new servant in hand and begins her training.

But Maggie was revising the script.

"I'm worth more than that," she said smartly.

"Yeah!" Jennifer yelled encouragement.

Captain Rowe raised his hand threateningly. "Hold your tongue, girl. I'll not be saddled with you. You go to whoever bids the highest." He turned back to the innkeeper. "Since I hear no other offers, Master Farthing . . ."

"Wait!"

The order came from a newcomer who'd just come aboard. "I'll double what's been bid."

It couldn't be! But the lurching of Eve's heart told her it was.

Vic pushed his way through the crowd. With a wicked

smile, he repeated his offer. Captain Rowe beckoned him to the forefront.

Eve was in shock. Vic's appearance was certainly not part of her revised script. What was he doing here? And looking so damn carefree?

As if by design, the clouds suddenly parted; through a streak of blue sky, a shaft of sunlight spotlighted the newcomer. In white sportshirt and dark pants, flashing a broad smile, Vic was every inch a hero come to the rescue. Maggie would be overjoyed at his appearance; Eve was confused.

The audience was tittering, enjoying the new challenge. Captain Rowe took the unexpected development in stride. "Well, now," the captain announced, "here's a visitor's taken a fancy to our Maggie. Where be your home, my good sir?"

"New York."

The captain frowned. "A colony not known to me. Is it near New Amsterdam, the Dutch settlement to the north?"

"They're one and the same."

"Not to my knowledge."

"Wait until 1664," Vic said with a grin.

The conversation continued, with Vic getting into the fun of it as Captain Rowe made him part of the play.

Eve's mind was in turmoil. Vic approached and stood next to her. "Why did you come here?" she asked, forgetting to stay in character.

"I've come for you." Humor softened the intensity of his gray eyes. "And it looks like I'm just in time," he added for the benefit of the audience. "I'd almost lost you."

There followed a rollicking harangue about price. The captain first rejected paper money and finally agreed to accept Vic's gold watch in payment.

"She's a willing worker and a good girl," Captain

Rowe told Vic. "Worth this generous price. But mind you, she's not to be ill used."

"I swear to treat her with the utmost tenderness."

"Ahah," cried Farthing, pointing an accusing finger. "He means to bed the girl."

"Is that true, sir? Do you have a lascivious purpose in mind?" Captain Rowe bellowed.

Vic didn't answer, but his smile was enough for Farthing. "You see," the innkeeper cried, "the man cannot deny it. His face marks his lechery. My bid is the more honorable one. If the girl works hard and gives good service, after her indenture, I will find her a decent farmer to wed."

"Best that offer," the captain challenged Vic.

"Yeah," Jennifer called amid a chorus of encouragement from others in the crowd.

Vic did. "I promise to marry her, not after seven years, but now. It's a wife, not a servant, I'm after."

"She's yours then," Captain Rowe declared. There were cheers and applause, even from the Sprays and the Farthings. They'd come out of character, realizing that what was happening here had more to do with Eve Marsdon than Maggie Tolliver.

Eve was still confused. Her head ached, her feet hurt. What was going on? Was this for real, or part of the pageant? She recovered sufficiently to smile and accept the congratulations of the visitors as they left the *Dove* to attend the next event. Jennifer, grinning with approval, held up her hand for a high five. "Way to go!" she cried.

Eve's mind was reeling. Go where?

He'd been right to come, Vic thought, keeping a tight hold on Eve's arm as he steered her toward a tree-shaded area away from the crowds. His first impulse had been to pick up the phone and call her from New York, but telephones were for business conversations and short messages, not for what he had to say to Eve.

Finding her had taken some doing. Loretta didn't know who the friends were that Eve had gone to. He'd finally gotten the Avedons' name from Glen Rader, but first had to endure Glen's jibes about Eve's apparently being dissatisfied enough to run out on Vic. He hadn't argued. How could he? It was true.

It was Greta Avedon who'd told him that Eve had gone home to Leonardtown.

"She doesn't want to see you," Greta had claimed.

Refusing to believe her, Vic had left for Leonardtown. He needed to see Eve, to explain and make her listen.

Then came the letdown of not finding her at home and fearing that his long drive had been futile . . . until he'd remembered his college friend, Eve's cousin Dave Bittner, who proved easy to locate and knew where Eve was.

Dave had mentioned the pageant, but Vic hadn't realized his meeting with Eve would have this unexpected seventeenth-century prologue. The sight of her back there on the *Dove*, so pert and saucy in her ill-fitting, bedraggled costume, filled his heart with love—and gratitude that he was free to claim her. Surely Eve guessed what he had to tell her. His happiness must give him away. Or would she be as surprised as he'd been at Maria's disclosure?

Maria had returned to New York and called him from her mother's.

"I know you've been trying to reach me," she'd told him. "Mom should never have left that message at your office, Vic. It must have blown your mind."

"It did, but it's all right."

"What's all right?"

He'd tried to sound accepting and positive. "That you're pregnant, that I'm going to be a father."

There was a pause, and then Maria had said, "Vic, please come over. We've got to talk."

Driving out to Brooklyn, he'd tried not to think about

Eve and what might have been. He forced himself to concentrate on what had to be.

Thankfully, Mama Spezia let her daughter and Vic talk privately. They sat together on the couch in the living room. Maria looked happier than he'd seen her for a long time.

"Pregnancy suits you," he said, trying to sound pleased.

"Yes. Who'd have thought it? Certainly not I."

Now came the important question. "What do you want to do?"

"Get married and have the baby," she replied instantly.

Vic took a deep breath. "Right. Then that's what we do."

Maria contemplated him with a wry smile and then relented. "I shouldn't do this to you." She gave his clenched hand a squeeze. "It's that streak of bitchiness in me that surfaces every once in a while. I just wanted to see what you'd say." Looking even happier, she leaned over and kissed his cheek. "But I've known you long enough to realize you'd say just exactly what you did. Vic, I'm sorry."

"What for? What are you talking about?"

"You don't have to marry me."

She made it sound like a reprieve. Vic was confused. "You're *not* pregnant?"

"I am. But not by you."

It took a while to sink in. Then suddenly it all fell into place—Mama Spezia's ambiguous message, Maria's visit to New Hampshire. Vic realized that in the back of his mind he'd hoped for something like this. "Frazier Doyle?"

"Frazier Doyle," Maria repeated happily.

Of course. Frazier's interest had been obvious. More than interest. Frazier loved Maria. She was going to have his baby.

"Do you love him?" he asked.

"Yes. It took a while for me to realize how much."

Great! Perfect! His tension drained. They hugged affectionately. Now Vic could honestly share Maria's joy.

They'd had a long talk, a belated admission of what they both had finally recognized. Like Vic, Maria had been reluctant to end their relationship and admit that it didn't fulfill her needs. She hadn't wanted to acknowledge that her needs had changed. She had blamed her tennis slump as the source of her disaffection. Not being able to slam through winning games as she once had was making her dissatisfied with her whole life.

But it was more than that, she eventually realized. Accepting the hard fact that it was time to retire from competitive play led to questions Maria hadn't known how to deal with—like, "What was next? Was there life after tennis stardom?"

Frazier Doyle had provided the answer.

From the first, Frazier had made his intentions clear. He wanted more than a brief affair. He saw Maria not as a tennis star and celebrity, but as a woman to share his life and have his children. If she loved him, she would have to accept what he was and what he wanted. Maria had drawn back, afraid of giving up her old life, and afraid of hurting Vic. It was Mrs. Spezia who'd suggested that, because of Eve, Vic might be experiencing the same kind of struggle. Learning she was carrying Frazier's child had brought everything into focus and forced her inevitable choice.

"I wasn't sure how to tell you," Maria said. "Mama said you'd be happy, but I can't help feeling guilty."

"Don't," Vic had told her. "Mama was right. I'm happy for you." *And for myself*, he'd added silently.

After saying good-bye, he'd had but one thought—to get to Eve. And here he was.

His arrival had been judiciously timed, he thought happily, to claim her publicly as his own. Playacting, but symbolic nevertheless. Eve, however, seemed angry. Was she still in the guise of the outspoken Maggie? Of course, she didn't yet know what Maria had told him.

Eve halted under a large maple tree. "Stop dragging me," she demanded.

There were so many emotions vying for ascendancy in her mind. At the moment, anger was the energizing force. Vic's part in that little drama was his own creation, not from a script. But what did it mean? Eve had been determined to put Vic Adesso out of her life. What right did he have showing up out of the blue like this, barging into her seventeenth-century refuge? And looking so damn pleased with himself!

"I'm not going one step further until you tell me what you're doing here."

"We need to talk," Vic said. "Why did you run away from me?"

"Why?" Such an unfeeling question. "You damn well know why."

"Tell me."

"Because there was no point in staying," she cried. "Because after what happened between us on the *Six Pack*, hearing that Maria was pregnant made me feel awful. I didn't want to be around when you talked to her. I didn't want to be in the way." She paused. More subdued, she asked, "Did you talk to her?"

"Yes."

"How is she?"

"Happy, and her mother's positively ecstatic."

Vic's smile was infuriating. "How nice!" Eve said. "How about you?"

"I'm happy for their sake."

Eve was stunned. Was he completely insensitive to her pain? But Vic wasn't like that. This whole scene had a surrealistic quality where truth and fantasy clashed. Wrenching away from his grasp, she stumbled out of Maggie's shoe. Vic caught her and held tight.

"Let me go."

"Never. Will you listen? I said I'm happy for *them*—for Maria and her mother and the baby." He paused before adding, "And especially for the baby's father—Frazier Doyle."

Eve's strength drained away with her anger. She fell limply against him. Vic gathered her closely in his arms. For a long moment, neither spoke. Then, his lips against her hair, Vic added the words she wanted to hear. "But most of all, I'm happy for us. We can be together. There's nothing to keep us apart. I love you, Eve." He waited, then asked, "Aren't you going to say something?"

From a flooding relief and happiness, Eve brought out a muffled "I love you, too."

"That's a start."

Eve pulled away to confront him. "But why did you tell me like this, going through that whole charade first?"

"I don't know. It just happened. Believe me, I didn't intend to get drawn into your pageant." He grinned. "It cost me an expensive wristwatch."

"You'll get it back." Her frustration gone, Eve could smile. She wanted to know more about his conversation with Maria. Vic gave her all the details.

When he'd finished, Vic, with a teasing glint in his eyes, said, "I must admit I kind of liked the idea of being a father."

"What?"

"But since I want children with curly black hair and green eyes," he hastened to add, "I'll have to have them with you."

"Will you now?" Eve asked with Maggie's jauntiness.

"But we'd better get married first. I gave my sworn word to the captain that I'd do the honorable thing."

"Don't I have a say in this?"

Vic became serious. "You do. Maggie was a bound servant. The woman I want to marry is free to choose her life." He gave her a tender smile. "What say you, Eve Marsdon? Will you have me?"

With a tremulous smile, she gave her answer. "I will."

Eve's emotions were again tumultuous, but this time joyously so. There were still many questions, and decisions to make. All in due time. Vic was here and they were free to love each other. That was enough for now. Eagerly, Eve welcomed his kiss.

They were oblivious to a passing couple of tourists. "Look, Max," the woman said to her husband. "Aren't they those actors from the boat? Maggie somethin' or other and the man who bid for her?"

"Looks like."

"D'you think they're still acting?"

"Don't look like no playacting to me." He smiled. "Sure looks like the real thing."

It surely was.

SHARE THE FUN . . .
SHARE YOUR NEW-FOUND TREASURE!!

You don't want to let your new books out of your sight? That's okay. Your friends can get their own. Order below.

No. 49 SUNLIGHT ON SHADOWS by Lacey Dancer
Matt and Miranda bring out the sunlight in each other's lives.

No. 50 RENEGADE TEXAN by Becky Barker
Rane lives only for himself—that is, until he meets Tamara.

No. 51 RISKY BUSINESS by Jane Kidwell
Blair goes undercover but finds more than she bargained for with Logan.

No. 52 CAROLINA COMPROMISE by Nancy Knight
Richard falls for Dee and the glorious Old South. Can he have both?

No. 53 GOLDEN GAMBLE by Patrice Lindsey
The stakes are high! Who has the winning hand—Jessie or Bart?

No. 54 DAYDREAMS by Marina Palmieri
Kathy's life is far from a fairy tale. Is Jake her Prince Charming?

No. 55 A FOREVER MAN by Sally Falcon
Max is trouble and Sandi wants no part of him. She *must* resist!

No. 56 A QUESTION OF VIRTUE by Carolyn Davidson
Neither Sara nor Cal can ignore their almost magical attraction.

No. 57 BACK IN HIS ARMS by Becky Barker
Fate takes over when Tara shows up on Rand's doorstep again.

No. 58 SWEET SEDUCTION by Allie Jordan
Libby wages war on Will—she'll win his love yet!

No. 59 13 DAYS OF LUCK by Lacey Dancer
Author Pippa Weldon finds her real-life hero in Joshua Luck.

No. 60 SARA'S ANGEL by Sharon Sala
Sara *must* get to Hawk. He's the only one who can help.

No. 61 HOME FIELD ADVANTAGE by Janice Bartlett
Marian shows John there is more to life than just professional sports.

No. 62 FOR SERVICES RENDERED by Ann Patrick
Nick's life is in perfect order until he meets Claire!

No. 63 WHERE THERE'S A WILL by Leanne Banks
Chelsea goes toe-to-toe with her new, unhappy business partner.

No. 64 YESTERDAY'S FANTASY by Pamela Macaluso
Melissa always had a crush on Morgan. Maybe dreams do come true!

No. 65 TO CATCH A LORELEI by Phyllis Houseman
Lorelei sets a trap for Daniel but gets caught in it herself.

No. 66 BACK OF BEYOND by Shirley Faye
Dani and Jesse are forced to face their true feelings for each other.

No. 67 CRYSTAL CLEAR by Cay David
Max could be the end of all Crystal's dreams . . . or just the beginning!

No. 68 PROMISE OF PARADISE by Karen Lawton Barrett
Gabriel is surprised to find that Eden's beauty is not just skin deep.

No. 69 OCEAN OF DREAMS by Patricia Hagan
Is Jenny just another shipboard romance to Officer Kirk Moen?

No. 70 SUNDAY KIND OF LOVE by Lois Faye Dyer
Trace literally sweeps beautiful, ebony-haired Lily off her feet.

No. 71 ISLAND SECRETS by Darcy Rice
Chad has the power to take away Tucker's hard-earned independence.

No. 72 COMING HOME by Janis Reams Hudson
Clint always loved Lacey. Now Fate has given them another chance.
